CRAZY
Connie's Closet

1959
A TIME TRAVEL SERIES

Janelle Otoya

ILLUMIFY
MEDIA.COM

Crazy Connie

Copyright © 2025 by Janelle A. Otoya

The views and opinions expressed in this book are those of the author and do not necessarily reflect the official policy or position of Illumify Media Global.

Published by

Illumify Media Global

www.IllumifyMedia.com

"Let's bring your book to life!"

Library of Congress Control Number: 2024924061

Paperback ISBN: 978-1-964251-29-5
Hardcover ISBN: 978-1-964251-30-1

Cover design by Debbie Lewis

Printed in the United States of America

To all the wonderful kids in my life.

Especially:
Katherine Rose
Brandon Michael
Sydney Elizabeth
Hayley Grace

Contents

Acknowledgements

Thank you to the Lord for blessing me with this book. To my family, especially Jose, Katie, Brandon, Mom, Jen, and Joelle for their unwavering love and support.

To my dear friend Annette. Thank you for reading and re-reading.

Larry Yoder, you are a book beast. That's all there is to say about that.

And to the Illumify family. Thank you for this great experience.

CHAPTER 1

Grandpa's Closet

Constance Pentori woke up in the bedroom where she always stayed when she visited Grandpa Tony. Mom said she could paint the walls whatever color she wanted now that they would be living there.

It was hard to imagine being here without Grandpa around. Her mind began to wander. Grandpa's funeral was yesterday, and the house had been full of people. It seemed like everyone from southeast Kansas had come to visit and eat. They had all brought yummy food too, like cakes and casseroles. Why was that?

Constance didn't understand it but was thankful for the chocolate cake with fluffy frosting that was in the kitchen. Maybe she could have a piece for breakfast. After all, Mom and Dad would be leaving for Italy this morning. They were taking Grandpa there to be buried next to Grandma. She laid there and thought about them, finally together again. Grandma had died when Constance was a baby.

"Oh, Grandpa," she said with a sigh. "I miss you already." She recalled the many wonderful visits she had made to this old house. She laughed, remembering the time they had gone fishing in the pond out back. Instead of a fish, though, she had caught a big bull frog. Grandpa had so much trouble getting it off the hook. He said he would fry it up for dinner, but she made him set it free.

"Guess it's just my pond now," Constance said sadly. She rolled over and snuggled her covers. There on her bedside table she saw the ashtray she had made Grandpa Tony at summer camp one year. Why had she made him an ashtray? Grandpa never smoked. But she remembered how he'd loved it when he opened it that Christmas. He'd kept his coins in there ever since.

"Morning, honey," Mom whispered as she came in and sat on the edge of her bed. She reached up and lightly brushed the hair off Constance's face. Constance closed her eyes, delighting in the way her mom's hands felt. "Not much of a birthday week, huh?" Grandpa had died the day after Constance turned eleven.

"It's okay," Constance replied. "It makes me feel good knowing he's with Grandma now. He always talked about the day he would see her again."

Tears welled up in her mother's eyes. "He loved you very much, sweetheart."

"I know, Mom." She sat up to give her mother a hug.

"Please be good for your brother. Aunt Jen will be here later this morning."

2

"Don't worry, Momma. I'll be fine," Constance reassured her as her dad walked into the room.

"We've got to get going, Gracie." He squeezed her mother's shoulders from behind and kissed her on the cheek. He then knelt on the floor beside Constance's bed and took her hand. "We'll be back before you know it, Con," he said lovingly. "I'm sorry to leave you like this. I know Anthony can be a dork," he teased with a smile, "but your brother loves you, and he will only be in charge until Aunt Jen gets here."

"Don't worry, Daddy. I'll be okay." She kissed and hugged him goodbye.

"I love you," he whispered into her ear. "I made you some pancakes downstairs."

"Yummy!" She smiled and threw her head back.

Her mother stopped in the doorway and turned back. "We'll call you later, honey."

"All right, Mom," she answered. "Don't forget to bring me back something cool!"

"And don't forget to say your prayers," her dad added.

"Okay, Daddy. Bye!" She laid back against her pillow for a good stretch.

What would life be like living here? Kansas City was a lot bigger than Pittsburg. Grandpa always reminded her that in Kansas there was no *h* at the end of Pittsburg like there was in Pittsburgh, Pennsylvania. She never knew why it mattered though. She'd always loved visiting Grandpa. They were great explorers! She smiled as she remembered the summer they had built a fort in the back pasture. Was it still there? She reached up and moved the curtain over the bed.

Rain? Oh, man! Stuck inside. Might as well go eat.

She kicked off the covers and headed downstairs for Dad's pancakes. He made the best. He said the trick was adding cinnamon and brown sugar. But Grandpa taught her the *real* trick. He always said, "The trick is to eat them just as the syrup begins to flirt with the pancakes." Constance knew that meant to eat them before the syrup was all soaked up!

As Constance warmed her pancakes in the microwave, she took tiny bites of the fluffy frosting. "Must be peanut butter in there," she said and poured herself a glass of milk. She glanced around for the teen magazine her mom had let her buy yesterday at the gas station, but she didn't see it. So she sat down and promptly ate her pancakes. When she had finished, she looked over at Grandpa's chair. "Hi Grandpa! I'm in your house but you're not here." She started to feel the sadness again, but then she heard Anthony coming down the hall.

"Oh yeh, yeh, yeh . . . she's my girl . . . yeh, yeh, yeh." He was listening to his headphones again. If only he could hear himself sing. He came into the kitchen and poured a bowl of cereal. As he returned the milk to the fridge, he spun around on one foot and pointed at his bowl. Dad was right. Anthony really was a dork. She rolled her eyes and squeezed past him to put her plate in the sink. He had been away at college for a whole year, and she wasn't so sure she was ready for him to be home all summer.

Anthony danced out of the room with his bowl, and she grabbed a paper plate off the stack. Her mouth watered as she cut herself a not-so-small piece of the chocolate cake. Boy, did it look good. It had two layers, and in between the two layers was more frosting.

Constance sat back down and took the first bite. *Now that's some crazy cake!* she thought as her chewing slowed and her eyes rolled back. She adored good food, especially dessert.

As she savored the cake, she imagined she was home alone. She couldn't wait until she was thirteen. That was how old her mom said she had to be before she didn't need a babysitter. Her other friends stayed by themselves all the time. But her mom was a little more strict. Constance didn't really mind, except for the staying-home-alone thing. It made her feel like a baby.

"Ugh!" She made a face and pushed her plate back. "I think I'm going to throw up!" she said. The cake was awesome, but her piece was too big! She scooted herself away from the table and slowly began to walk back up to her room, stopping in the den. She had never noticed it before, but her first-grade picture was framed on top of the television. Grandpa had pulled her front tooth the weekend before that picture was taken. He told her he just wanted to feel how loose it was. Before she knew it, he was holding her tooth in his hand. The tooth fairy left two silver dollars that night.

Grandpa also had pictures hung all along the hallway, mostly of her mom and her grandma. They were both so pretty. Constance reached up and touched the picture of Grandma holding her the day she was born. Mom had always told her how thankful she was that Grandma got to meet Constance before she had died.

The smell of Grandpa filled the hallway as she passed his room. She would explore in there later. This would be the first time she had been left to explore the house alone. Sure, Anthony was home, but he would stay in his room or in the kitchen. Usually, Mom and Grandpa were never too far away, and they always set her boundaries. The little closet in Grandpa's room? Off-limits! That was where he kept his shotgun. His top dresser drawer was also off-limits. He kept important papers there. He had been shocked the day Constance found his passport under his bed.

Constance was certain that her mother hid things on purpose around the house to make her visits more exciting. One time she found an old case full of Fashion Girl clothes. It was in the dresser of the room where she stayed. *Her* room now. It was Mom's room when she was growing up.

Constance loved Fashion Girls. Her mom did too. A lot of Constance's friends said they were too old for Fashion Girls, but she disagreed. She loved dressing them up and doing their hair, pretending they were going somewhere exciting and glamorous. Her mom always teased Constance because she had about fifteen Fashion Girl dolls. Mom said she only had two when she was young: a blonde and a brunette. If she wanted one to go to the beach, she'd just put her in a swimsuit instead of buying the special version that came with the bikini and surfboard.

On one visit to Grandpa's, Constance found her mom's high school senior yearbook on the top shelf of her closet. Her mom thought it was lost and was thrilled when Constance found it. They sat and looked at it for hours.

That was one place Constance loved to explore: the big closet. It was amazing and cluttered with clothes, shoes, and other stuff that didn't have a home. It was shaped like a rectangle and was fairly deep. Grandpa had several shoe racks lined up in the far back.

Mom worried about her exploring in the back corner. She told Constance there might be spiders hiding there. Consequently, Constance was not allowed to go past the first row of shoe racks. Even then, the closet was awesome! Grandpa was constantly tossing things in there to get them out of the way. She would always show her discoveries to her mom, who generally knew what they were, and to whom they belonged. She also knew if there was a story behind them.

One of Constance's favorite finds was an old shoe box of pictures that even Mom had never seen. They were photographs of Grandma and Grandpa growing up. There were photos of their parents and even photos of Grandma and Grandpa while they were dating. She didn't find any wedding pictures, but there were some marked "Honeymoon." Mom took the box and put them in a scrapbook for Grandpa. She gave it to him for his birthday one year, and everyone cried when he opened it.

Once, Constance even found a ruby ring in the closet. She was on her knees and saw it way in the back. Technically, she didn't go beyond her boundaries because her knees stayed where they were supposed to; it was the rest of her body that she stretched as far as she could. She couldn't believe her luck when she finally had it in her hands.

The ring looked very old, so she figured it must have been Grandma's. She couldn't wait to show it to her mother. It must have been really special to Grandma because when she showed it to her mother, she started to cry. Constance asked if it was Grandma's, but her mother didn't answer. She asked her mother if she could have it, but her mother quickly answered no. She told Constance that the ring was more precious than she would ever know. Maybe one day when she was older it could be hers. But not until then.

Older. Constance always had to be *older.*

Constance went back to her room and sat down on the bed with a sigh. Even though Mom and Dad were gone, she figured she should probably go ahead and get dressed. Her mom always teased that Constance would go to school in her pajamas if they would let her. With the right pajamas, that was probably true.

Constance threw on some play clothes with the hope that it would stop raining soon. If it did, she could ride her bike down to Mr. Marshall's house. Grandpa had told her last week on the phone about the new horse Mr. Marshall had bought, and she couldn't wait to see it. Mr. Marshall taught Constance to ride horses when she was about five, and she had been riding ever since. He and Grandpa were good friends. She didn't remember seeing him yesterday at the funeral, but the whole day seemed kind of blurry.

She plopped down on her bed to pack a few things into her backpack. She liked to be prepared when she went exploring. She had learned that from her mom. Mom was the greatest about being prepared. No matter how small the purse, she always had whatever was needed. Band-Aid? Check! First-aid ointment? Check! Tissues? Hand wipes? Dental floss? In the side pocket. She always had a bottle of water in case Constance got thirsty and fruit snacks if she wanted a treat.

"Let's see . . . What will I need?" Constance said. "Purple nail polish for sure. My Fashion Girl flashlight for all the dark, spooky places." She made herself laugh at that thought. "Sneakers? Nope, too big for the bag. Flip-flops? Yes, perfect." Her eyes caught sight of something. "Hey, my magazine!" It was there on the floor. Then she saw the big bag of chocolate candies a lady from Grandpa's church had brought yesterday. *Thank you very much. Oops! Better bring something to drink.* She grabbed a bottle of water from the dresser and stuck it in her pack.

Constance wondered what Grandpa and Mom had stashed in the room as she slowly looked around. She remembered the time she found an old baseball glove under the bed. Suddenly, she flopped over the side—her feet still on top—as her head dangled to the floor to peek underneath. "Nope, nothing under there," she said, seeing only old wrapping paper and her suitcase. She sat back up and faced the closet. "Yes!" she said. She hopped off the bed and slowly danced over.

As always, Constance was amazed when she opened the door. It was big and deep with rows of clothes hanging on both sides. She held out her hands and touched them all as she made her way to the first row of shoe racks. She looked around in awe and pulled the metal chain to turn on the light. There were so many pairs of shoes and boots. Most of them looked like Grandpa's old work boots. But wait! Out of the corner of her eye she spied something bright and shiny. It was a box wrapped in lavender paper and tied with a yellow bow—all the way in the back corner. She hesitated for a moment, looked around for spiders, then carefully tiptoed back to it. "Crazy!" she said, seeing her name on the card. "My birthday! Thank you, Grandpa!" She sat on the floor of the closet and slid the card from the envelope. A twenty-dollar bill fell into her lap! "Ah, Gramps! You rock!" She gripped the money in her fist and stuck it in the front pocket of her backpack.

In the card he had written: *I hope this gift takes you on many great adventures.*

She hugged the box close as she leaned against the closet wall. "Ah Graaaaammmmpppss!" Suddenly, the closet wall gave way, and Constance tumbled down, down, down through darkness until she landed with a thud!

CHAPTER 2

Aunt Sylvi's Closet

"**O**uch!" *What happened? What's that smell? Furniture polish? Why is it so dark? Am I hurt?*

"Ahh!" someone yelled, and it wasn't Constance!

"Ahh!" Constance yelled back, scrambling as far from the voice as she could. Oh my goodness! Oh my goodness!

Suddenly, a light came on. There, in front of Constance, stood a boy!

"Ahh!" Constance screamed again, this time even louder. *Where are all of Grandpa's clothes?*

"Who are you?" they both screamed in unison.

"I asked you first!" they both replied.

"Listen, pal!" Constance held up karate-chop hands. "I took karate for two summers at the YMCA, and if you don't get out of here right this minute, I'm going to kick your—"

"Be my guest!" the boy quickly interrupted, then threw open the door. Was he mad? Was he dangerous? How did he get in here?

"You first," Constance said cautiously, still poised for karate chopping. "And no sudden moves."

"What is this? A stickup?" The boy chuckled as he put his hands above his head and walked out of the closet.

"Very funny!" Constance followed him out, then quickly jumped past him. She watched him cautiously from the corner of her eye. "Now who are you and what are you doing in . . ." Her voice trailed off as she looked around and began to realize that she wasn't at her grandpa's house anymore. "This is crazy," she whispered.

"What am *I* doing in *my* Aunt Sylvi's hall closet?" the boy muttered, a bit offended. "What I'm doing here is really none of your business. But if you must know, I was hiding from the Indians. Ya see—the boy swayed back and forth, then put his thumbs in his pockets—"I'm the sheriff in these here parts."

He's nuts! Constance thought. She noticed the boy was wearing a big belt with two pretend pistols in holsters on his hips. This had to be a crazy dream.

"What's wrong with you?" she demanded.

"What do you mean 'what's wrong with me'?" He walked back into the closet and looked around. "Where did you come from?"

"What's with the outfit?" she asked, still keeping her distance.

"Outfit? I'm playing Cowboys and Indians. *Bang! Bang!*" he cried as he whipped out the pistols and pointed them at Constance.

Yeah, he's completely nutzo, Constance thought as she looked around and followed him through a doorway. This must be his bedroom.

"You don't play Cowboys and Indians?" The boy tossed his pretend pistols on the bed. "Where are you from? The moon or something?"

"No! Pittsburg, Kansas," Constance replied with a smirk. "Thank you very much!" Her eyes anxiously scanned the room.

"No kidding?" he asked excitedly and spun around to face Constance. "I'm from Frontenac, Kansas."

"Is that close?" She noticed several stacks of comic books in the corner.

"Close? Why, we're practically neighbors! I'm Joseph Gordano. Pleased to make your acquaintance." He extended his hand to Constance.

Constance shook his hand reluctantly. "Um, I'm Constance Pentori. And *HELLOO,* where am I?" Maybe she had fallen and hit her head or something. She had seen that happen once in a movie. A guy hit his head and dreamed he was walking on train tracks for three days.

"Well, Constance Pentori..." Joseph trailed off as he flopped onto his bed. "I think I'll call you Connie. You see, Connie, you are at my Aunt Sylvi's house on 179 Third Street, St. Louis, Missouri, on this the first day of my summer vacation, June 5, 1959! And I thought this summer would be a drag," he added as he laid back and tossed a baseball in the air. "My friends back home are never going to believe this!"

"That's crazy," Constance muttered. She suddenly felt sick. "Something's not right here. 1959?" She sat down on a chair beside his desk. "That's impossible. I was born in 1995!" She looked up at Joseph. "Something is definitely not right!"

Joseph looked startled. "1995? Whoa! You *are* from the moon or something!" He stared blankly at her as the baseball crashed down on his face.

"Ow!" he cried and sat up on his bed, then cupped his hand around his nose.

"Holy cow! You're bleeding!" Constance panicked and began hopping from one foot to the next. "What do I do? What do I do?"

"Aunt Sylvi," Joseph said calmly as he continued to hold his nose. "Don't worry. We'll get Aunt Sylvi. She always knows what to do."

With that, Constance followed Joseph down a long wooden staircase. "What if she thinks I hit you?"

"Nah. You look too nice for that."

"Well, there is that karate thing."

"Yeah." Joseph paused at the end of the staircase and whispered, "Terrifying."

"You *should* be terrified!" Constance followed him into the kitchen. "*Sheriff*," she mumbled smugly.

They found his Aunt Sylvi at the kitchen counter. "Aunt Sylvi," Joseph said calmly, "we have a problem."

Aunt Sylvi turned to find Joseph's hands and face covered in blood. "Oh, we certainly do, dear," she said with a fright, then scrambled to wash her hands.

"Oh, I don't mean me!" Joseph replied. "I just need a rag and some ice. I mean *we* have a problem. Sylvi Gordano, meet Connie. She just fell out of the ceiling in the upstairs closet. She lives in Pittsburg, Kansas, and says she was born in 1995."

"Oh, good golly!" Aunt Sylvi ran to a drawer and handed Joseph a towel. "Are you hurt, dear?" she asked Constance, without really noticing her.

Constance exhaled. "No, I think I'm okay." She sat down at the kitchen table. "A little shook up maybe. My name is Constance, by the way, not Connie." She smirked at Joseph, who now sat across the table from her.

Aunt Sylvi grabbed a few pieces of ice and handed them to Joseph.

"Mrs. Gordano, do you think you can help me get home?" Constance asked, resting her forehead on the table.

"Oh, of course, dear," she assured Constance. "And do call me Aunt Sylvi, love." Putting her fingers under his chin, Aunt Sylvi lifted Joseph's face and gave him a good looking over. She was a plump old woman who seemed more like a grandma than an aunt. Constance liked her instantly.

Together they cleaned up Joseph's face, and Constance told them about the big move her family had just made into her grandpa's house. She explained that he had recently died and her parents were in Italy for a trip. She told them how she had planned a big day of exploring when she found a birthday present in her grandpa's closet.

"I just turned eleven. I thought Grandpa missed my birthday. But sure enough, he had a present ready and waiting for me. It was so crazy! All I did was lean against the closet wall, and before I knew it I was in your closet upstairs. Crazy! Absolutely crazy!"

"Wait! My present. I was holding it when I fell, and my backpack." She looked at Joseph. "Do you think they traveled here with me?"

"Who knows? I don't even know how *you* got here! But don't move. I'll go check." Joseph jumped up from the table and walked quickly toward the stairs.

"You know, Miss Constance"—Aunt Sylvi reached across the table and took her hand—"since we missed your birthday, tonight I will bake you a grand cake. You can come back tomorrow after dinner to celebrate. You *can* come back tomorrow, right?" Aunt Sylvi returned to the tomatoes she had been slicing before Constance could answer. "Would you like to stay for dinner tonight, dear?"

Uh-oh, Constance thought. *Aunt Sylvi's not with the program.* Had she not heard what Joseph said about her being from the future? Or was the woman just a little crazy? *Where did Joseph go?*

"Sure. Thank you. I'll stay for dinner. That would be great." Constance wished Joseph would return. "I think I'll go see if I can help Joseph."

"Okay, dear. We're having lasagna. Should be ready about five-thirty," Aunt Sylvi called as Constance rushed from the room.

Maybe telling Aunt Sylvi wasn't such a good idea after all. This was terrible!

"Joseph!" Constance cried when she saw him come down the stairs. "Your Aunt Sylvi doesn't get it! She just asked if I could come back tomorrow for birthday cake! What are we going to do? Who is going to help me get home?" She buried her face in her hands and sank down on the steps. Joseph sat down beside her.

"Don't worry, Connie. We'll figure it out. We just have to go back in there and *make* her understand." He calmly placed the purple box and her backpack on the next step down.

"But how?" Constance felt very frustrated. "I just turned eleven. I'm not even good at being eleven yet. What if she thinks I'm just telling a big story? Oh, I have to pray!" She quickly clasped her hands together and bowed her head.

Joseph sat there in silence until she had finished. He wasn't sure what she had prayed for, but somehow he felt better. He reached down and lifted her backpack. "So, what's in your satchel?" he asked. "Maybe something in here will convince my aunt."

"Not much." Constance took her bag from him and unzipped it. "Some purple nail polish." She pulled it out of her bag.

"Boy! That's awful!" Joseph examined the bottle. "Purple fingernails? Girls really do that?"

"They do, and I love it!" She yanked the bottle way from him, set it on the step, and took a moment to admire her recently painted toenails. "I have a Fashion Girl flashlight." She handed it to him.

"Hmm. Interesting," Joseph mumbled. He had flashlights for camping and working on the house, but he had never seen one made for girls. He examined it and flicked it on and off, on and off.

"Flip-flops." Constance took them out and put them on her bare feet. "Chocolate candies!" She held up the bag.

"Jeepers!" Joseph took the bag with both hands. He held it like the finest gold. "Where did you get the gigantic bag?" he asked in awe. "Can I open it?"

"Sure," she said as she dug deeper into her backpack. "Only other thing I have is a bottle of water." She handed it to him as well.

"Neat," he said around a mouthful of chocolate. "You put your water in a bottle? That's a good idea. It's like a canteen."

"It's not a canteen! We buy it like that." Connie gave him a questioning look.

"Really? Why? Don't you have faucets?" Joseph questioned.

She rolled her eyes. "Don't be crazy. Of course we have faucets."

"Then why do you buy your water in a bottle?"

She thought for a moment. "I don't really know. Hey, wait! I do have a magazine and some money that my grandpa gave me. But that's it." She reached in her bag and pulled out her teen magazine. On the front cover were models in silver jumpsuits with blue lipstick and blue hair extensions.

"Is this a space magazine?" Joseph asked as he looked at the cover.

"What do you mean? No!" Constance snapped. "It's just a magazine for girls. It's about life."

"Whose life?" Joseph asked under his breath. He took the magazine from her and examined it further. He didn't completely understand what it was about. Suddenly, he yelled, "That's it! She has to believe us! It says right here 'May 2006.' Gee, that looks crazy."

Yeah, crazy, Constance thought. How was she ever going to get out of here? She took the magazine from Joseph. "I guess it could work." She shrugged. This issue looked like a good one. She took a second to flip through the pages.

"Let's go," he said. With a plan, they headed back to the kitchen and sat at the table. Constance decided to let Joseph do all the talking.

"Okay, Aunt Sylvi, we have something important to tell you."

"Go ahead, dear." Aunt Sylvi turned to face them while wiping her hands on her apron.

"All right," Joseph said with a sigh. "Okay, you know Connie here, right? Well, she's eleven, right? Just turned eleven."

"Constance!" Constance corrected.

"Yes, dear." Aunt Sylvi nodded. "Constance. Eleven."

"Well, she was born in the year 1995, Aunt Sylvi. *Nineteeeeen Niiinty-Fiiive.* That means where she lives is the year 2006. *Twooo thowsand and* six. She's a time traveler, Aunt Sylvi. *A time traveler!*

Aunt Sylvi looked at Joseph. "I'm sorry, dear, I don't quite understand."

Connie handed Joseph the magazine, and he in turn handed it to Aunt Sylvi. "This is her magazine. She had it in her bag. Have a look at the date on the cover."

She took the magazine and began to look it over. Joseph and Constance looked at each other with anticipation. Aunt Sylvi looked up at them and with a chuckle said, "You crazy kids! You almost got me on that one!" She tossed it back on the table and turned around.

"Wait!" Constance cried. She remembered a picture she had seen in the magazine. "Has the movie *Summer Love* been out yet?" It was a favorite of Grandpa's, she recalled.

"Oh yes, dear. With that darling Liza LaRue," Aunt Sylvi crooned. Joseph rolled his eyes.

"Yes," Constance continued, "Liza LaRue! You know who she is?" She nodded to Aunt Sylvi.

21

"Of course, dear. Such a pretty girl. And what a figure!" Aunt Sylvi smiled. Joseph made a grossed-out face.

"How old would you say she is, Aunt Sylvi?" Constance persisted.

"Oh, twenty or so. Why do you ask?"

"Yeah, why do you ask?" Joseph questioned.

"Just wait!" Constance snapped at him and directed her attention back to Aunt Sylvi. She knew this was her only chance. "So if this magazine was, in fact, written in 2006, how old would Liza LaRue be today?"

"Oh, goodness me! That's nearly fifty years. She'd be almost seventy years old," Aunt Sylvi calculated.

Connie flipped to a picture in the magazine and showed it to Joseph. "Yikes!" he grimaced.

Liza LaRue was an old actress who had not aged well. Her face had become wrinkled, and she wore way too much makeup. Frankly, Miss LaRue looked downright scary. Constance got up from the table. She handed the magazine back to Aunt Sylvi and pointed out the picture.

Aunt Sylvi studied it for several minutes. She looked back at the date on the front cover. Slowly, she looked at Constance with a blank stare and suddenly fell to the floor.

"Holy cow!" Constance screamed and looked at Joseph.

"She fainted!" Joseph said as they ran to her.

"Aunt Sylvi! Aunt Sylvi!" They shouted and tried to wake her up. *Oh, this is terrible, just terrible,* Constance thought.

Aunt Sylvi's eyes blinked once and then again. When she finally opened them, she reached out to touch Constance's cheek. "You poor, dear child. You must be scared to pieces." Joseph helped Aunt Sylvi sit back up. "I don't understand how this has happened, but I promise I'll do everything I can to get you back home."

"Oh, thank you." Constance hugged Aunt Sylvi tightly. "Thank you so much!"

With that, Joseph helped Aunt Sylvi to her feet. "Well, that fixes it," she said decidedly as she brushed herself off and straightened her apron. "Tomorrow morning I'm off to the library! We're going to figure this out." She walked unsteadily to the sink. "Oh my!" She turned back to Connie. "You're going to need some clothes, and I have the perfect idea!" She dumped her tomatoes into a pot. "Joseph's Aunt Tini brought by some of his cousin Marie's old clothes. I'm going to take them to the church bazaar next month. They should be about your size." She opened the refrigerator and leaned into it. "I put them in an old box up in the attic. Why don't you two go see if you can find it? It's marked 'St. Andrew's Bazaar.'"

"Wow! The attic!" Joseph exclaimed. "Let's go!" He ran for the stairs.

"Wait!" Constance called. She stopped to grab her backpack and all of her stuff, including the birthday present from Grandpa that was still unopened.

CHAPTER 3

The Attic

Joseph ran up the long wooden staircase, down the hall, around the corner, and up five more stairs to get to the attic. "Whoa!" he said and stopped suddenly when he reached the top. "Look at all this stuff!"

"Crazy," Constance said as she ran into his back. "Sorry." They both looked around in amazement. It was a spacious room with a slanted ceiling. It smelled like the trunk Grandpa kept at the foot of his bed. There were five large windows that nearly reached the floor: two on each side and one in the back. On one side of the room were many boxes stacked around; on the other side were several large objects covered with what looked like white bed sheets. She put her things down.

They ran to look out the windows. They could see all the way down Aunt Sylvi's street and practically right into the neighbor's house. Joseph explained that a man and a woman lived there. Sometimes the man would come out and play stick ball with Joseph and the neighborhood gang, but they didn't have any kids of their own.

Joseph pulled off the sheets and discovered a soft, red sofa with a matching chair, two small tables, and one big table. He promptly parked himself on the sofa.

"A little dusty," Constance remarked as she waved away the dust cloud. She picked up one of the sheets and folded it. After a few minutes she decided to just wad them up and make a pile. While tossing them on the floor, she noticed a big box marked "St. Andrew's Bazaar" against the wall. "Do you suppose that's the box with the clothes for me?"

"Looks like it." Joseph leaned sideways to see around Constance.

She opened it and rummaged through the contents.

"Mind if I have a look at your magazine?" Joseph asked as she held up a green-and-orange striped shirt.

"Sure."

He reached for the backpack. As he unzipped it, the big bag of chocolate candies fell out. "Oh, can I have more of your chocolate? *Please*?"

Constance didn't even look up. "Sure, help yourself." She began to realize that most of the shirts in the box were striped. Not that there was anything wrong with stripes; she just thought it was odd. She made herself laugh as she thought about it. *Maybe that's why they were going to the bazaar . . . because they are bizarre!* She cracked herself up! *That's classic!*

Joseph grabbed more candy. "Hey, there are blue ones in here!"

"You don't have blue ones?" Constance asked over her shoulder.

"Nope." His mouth was full as he shook his head.

How crazy! Were things really this different fifty years ago?

Constance continued to dig through the clothes until she found a really cute sweater. It was soft and pink and had little beaded flowers on it. But it was summertime. What good was a sweater going to do her, no matter how cute it was?

"It's really nice of your Aunt Sylvi to let me borrow these clothes, but I have to say, they look kind of dorky." She pulled out a pair of tennis shoes and replaced her flip-flops with them. "Hey, these fit!"

"What do you mean *dorky*?" he asked and peered over the top of the magazine.

"You know, geeky. Like a geek," she explained unsuccessfully.

Joseph stared at her blankly with raised eyebrows.

"Like a nerd."

"Oh yeah. Kind of," he remarked and returned to the magazine. "Cousin Marie's nice, but I don't know about her taste in fashion. Says here in the magazine that 'pink is the new black.'"

"Really?" Constance chuckled. "I've got some fashion for you." She pulled out a rather large bra and put it on over her shirt. She turned around to face Joseph and posed like a supermodel. "What do you think of this?"

Joseph laid the magazine on his chest and looked up. "What are you doing?" he screamed. He squeezed his eyes shut and threw his arms up to block his face. "Get that off! Come on! That's Cousin Marie's! Ew!"

"Yes, well it looks like Cousin Marie is quite a healthy girl." Constance laughed and did one last little dance.

"Come on! I said get it off!"

Constance laughed harder and continued to check out the rest of the clothes. After she had dug as deep as she could, she found some headbands she liked and a couple pairs of shorts that weren't too bad. She also discovered some nightgowns - two were long and one was really short with matching poofy underwear or something. She didn't like the short one, but she was six the last time she had a long night gown, and she thought these were pretty. She pulled them out with a few outfits and piled them on the steps to take downstairs.

Slowly, she began to pull off more sheets. "Hey, check out this desk . . . and this chair! This is awesome! I love chairs that spin." Constance sat down and took it for a ride. It wobbled a little, but it was still neat.

"What does that mean, 'pink is the new black'?" Joseph asked, still deeply involved in her magazine.

"I don't know. I guess it means pink matches everything," she answered as she looked through the desk drawers.

"Really? I don't think so," Joseph disagreed.

"Cool!" Constance exclaimed. "Look at this eraser! Grandpa had one like this that he let me use one time when I was drawing."

Joseph closed the magazine and propped himself up with his elbows. "So, tell me more about yourself, Connie."

She giggled a little and moved from the desk to the red chair. "Well, I like to ride bikes. My favorite color is purple."

"Favorite food?" Joseph asked quickly.

"Pancakes."

"Favorite cookie?"

"Chocolate chip."

"What do you want to be when you grow up?"

"Hm, that's a hard one," Constance answered. "Not sure yet. Something exciting. Okay, now you!" She folded her legs in the chair. "Favorite color?"

"Red."

"Food?"

"Orange Popsicles. I love 'em! I always eat the orange ones first."

"Hmm. Strange. Cookie?"

"Snickerdoodles."

"Oh! I like those too! And when you grow up?" Constance prodded.

"Easy. A writer!" Joseph exclaimed.

"Like a book writer or a newspaper writer?"

"I don't really know," he said. "Books, I think." He rolled onto his stomach. "What do you say we ask Aunt Sylvi if this can be our hangout? I like it up here."

"Me too." She leaned back in the chair and looked around. "But I'm not staying long, remember? We have to find a way for me to get home tomorrow."

"We'll figure it out," Joseph said confidently. "Aunt Sylvi's going to the library, right? And you and I can investigate the closet completely. Aunt Sylvi's got bikes we can ride up to Simpson's Dime Store and see if they have any magnifying glasses. We'll be true detectives!" Connie was starting to believe that Joseph just might be able to get her home. "We can start our own detective agency. We'll call it 'Pentori and Gordano, Private Eyes!' We'll get some paints and make a sign and hang it right there." He motioned toward the staircase, then changed the subject and rolled back over to look at her. "Say, Connie, why don't you open your present?"

"Wow, I almost forgot!" Constance jumped up excitedly to retrieve her slightly battered box. As she unwrapped it, she told Joseph about the great presents her grandpa always gave her and the many adventures they'd had together. Her favorite present, she explained, was the Elmo fishing pole he had given her when she was five. That was the year he taught her to fish.

"What's an Elmo fishing pole?" Joseph asked.

"You know, a fishing pole with a handle that looks like Elmo."

"Who's Elmo?" he persisted.

"He's a puppet on *Sesame Street*." She could not believe he didn't know who Elmo was.

"Where's Sesame Street? Is that in Pittsburg?" he asked, confused.

"Pittsburg? No! It's a TV show!"

"Hm," Joseph said, "never heard of it."

"Crazy!" Constance shook her head in disbelief. She was beginning to feel a little homesick. She opened her present slowly. Inside she found a black case with round edges.

"What is it?" Joseph tried to take a peek.

"I don't know." She examined the case. There was a zipper that ran around the top. She unzipped it cautiously to find a pair of shiny black binoculars inside. "Crazy!" She pulled them out carefully. "Binoculars!" Without a thought, she held them up and took a look at Joseph.

"Golly, Connie! Let's try 'em out!" He motioned for Connie to follow him. They ran to the far window and dropped to their knees. Constance took the first turn. "These are great! I can see all the way down Aunt Sylvi's street!" She looked around at all the houses. They were brick and seemed to sit very close together. Each of them had a neat porch that Constance had heard Aunt Sylvi call the "stoop." Nobody she knew at home ever said *stoop*. She liked it.

She took a peek in the neighbor's window. It looked like an office or something. She could also see a gum wrapper that was left on their stoop. She could almost read it. "Wow!" Constance exclaimed. "These are great! There's a guy walking down the sidewalk. I can even read the name on his shirt! His name is . . . Oops! Hang on! He moved." She paused for a second to look over the top of the binoculars so she could find him again. With one more look she said, "Vincent. His name is Vincent. Crazy!"

"Vincent? That's Uncle Gordy! Can I have a look?" he asked as she handed over the binoculars. Uncle Gordy was Aunt Sylvi's son, Joseph explained. He worked at the filling station. Last summer he had a different job, and he had been a lot nicer then. "Yep, that's Uncle Gordy all right! He lives here with Aunt Sylvi. He's usually a lot of fun when I stay for the summer. But when I got here last night, he seemed different." He handed Constance the binoculars.

"Different, how?" Constance asked. "And is his name Vincent or Gordy?"

"Vincent Gordano. Gordy for short."

"I see. Well, maybe he's just not feeling well, or he's having a bad day or something." She took another turn and looked out the window again. "Or maybe it's because two mean-looking guys are yelling at him!"

"What?" Joseph grabbed the binoculars from Constance. A big black car was driving slowly alongside Uncle Gordy, but he kept his head down and walked briskly down the sidewalk. Joseph could see two men in the front seat. The passenger was leaning out the window, shaking his fist at Gordy. "Gee, they sure do look mad!" Joseph exclaimed.

"Do you think he's in some sort of trouble?" Constance asked, concerned.

"I don't know, but let's go see. He's walking up the stoop now." Connie and Joseph dashed down the steps, around the corner, through the hall, and down the big wooden staircase. They reached the bottom just as Uncle Gordy threw open the door. His work boots made a loud thud on the hardwood floor.

"Hey, Uncle Gordy. Are you doing okay?" Joseph asked. Gordy did not stop. "I want you to meet my new friend, Connie—"

"Get lost, kid," Gordy interrupted. He marched down the hall and slammed his bedroom door.

"Well he's not very nice at all!" Constance exclaimed, looking at Joseph.

"Like I said"—Joseph lowered his head sadly— "he's different lately."

"Do you think we should tell your Aunt Sylvi?" she asked, still worried.

"No, but we can go see if she's got anything to eat." Joseph led the way to the kitchen. Constance thought it was remarkable how he could instantly switch from sadness to food. "We can ask about the attic too," he added.

"Are you always that distracted by food?" Constance asked.

"What do you mean?"

"Well, thirty seconds ago you were all bummed out about your uncle. Now you are looking for something to eat."

"Oh, that." He chuckled. "That just happens when I get close to Aunt Sylvi's kitchen."

"You know, it does smell really great down here!" Constance smiled and took a deep breath.

"Aunt Sylvi is swell! You're going to want to stay forever!"

Forever? she thought. *Will I ever go home?* The idea made her feel sick. She was thankful to be here with Joseph and Aunt Sylvi, but she longed to be back at Grandpa's house. *Her* house.

As they entered the kitchen the aroma got stronger and stronger. Aunt Sylvi was busy with something in the oven. A big loaf of fresh-baked crusty bread sat on the countertop. "Mmm. Bread!" Joseph inhaled and hovered over the loaf. "Can we have a little? Please?"

"Just a little, dear," Aunt Sylvi answered. "But save some for dinner."

Joseph tore two large pieces from the end of the loaf. He juggled them a little as they were still steaming hot. Quickly, he handed a chunk to Constance, and they both began to blow on their pieces. When they finally tasted the bread, they closed their eyes and chewed slowly to savor every bite.

"This is heaven," Constance complimented. Aunt Sylvi seemed pleased.

"Why don't you two set the table? Vincent is going out, so it will just be the three of us. The tablecloth is in the top drawer of the dining room hutch. Why don't you use the blue-flowered dishes?"

"You bet!" Constance replied. "Let's go!" She grabbed Joseph's hand and pulled him into the dining room. They found the hutch where Aunt Sylvi kept the tablecloths and other table linens. She couldn't believe how many tablecloths Aunt Sylvi had. There were white ones, green ones, blue ones, red ones, flowered ones, and lace ones. She decided since they were using the white dishes with the blue flowers, that she would pick the blue tablecloth with white fringe. She pulled out three matching cloth napkins as well.

The dishes were in the top half of the hutch. The ones with blue flowers were delicate. Connie handled them carefully. Joseph set out the silverware and filled the glasses with water.

Soon Aunt Sylvi brought in the platters of food: lasagna on one platter and corn on the cob on another. There was something Constance didn't recognize and, of course, the loaf of crusty bread. Aunt Sylvi situated herself in her chair and asked Joseph to say the blessing. He smiled and bowed his head. "Dear Lord, thank You for this wonderful meal and the wonderful hands that prepared it. Lord, thank You for Connie. Please help her get home safely, and please be with Uncle Gordy too. Amen."

"Thank you, Joseph," Aunt Sylvi said and passed the corn to Constance. "Now eat up before things get cold." Aunt Sylvi continued to pass all of the food to her. Once Constance had taken her serving, she promptly handed the platters across the table to Joseph. Aunt Sylvi passed her the dish she did not recognize. She smiled and took a small portion.

As she handed the plate to Joseph, he said, "Gee, Connie, is that all you're going take? I love fried eggplant! I could eat the whole plateful!"

"Eggplant," Constance pondered. "Interesting." Her mom had fixed some dishes with eggplant in them, but she had never seen it prepared like this before. She cautiously took a bite. Not bad! Not bad at all! She reached across the table for Joseph to pass it back. "Hey! Don't take it all!" she joked.

Everyone settled into their meal. For a moment, all that could be heard was the sound of silverware clinking against the plates.

Joseph wiped lasagna from his chin and broke the silence. "Say, Aunt Sylvi, Connie and I are going to start a detective agency tomorrow to investigate how she can get home. Can we use the attic as our hangout?"

"Why sure, dear," Aunt Sylvi said and broke off a piece of bread. "It's a bit of a mess up there. Do be careful."

"Oh, we will!" Joseph assured her. "And we'll fix it up good! Mind if we take the bikes up to the dime store tomorrow to get some supplies?" He concentrated on his ear of corn.

"Goodness me! What kind of supplies do you think you'll need?" Aunt Sylvi got up to retrieve a pitcher of water to refill the glasses.

"You know, basic things. Magnifying glasses, paint to make a sign. Stuff like that."

"And I have money," Constance chimed in. "You won't have to buy a thing!"

"That's nice, dear. But you save your money. I'm happy to give you a few dollars. Tell you what. I'll give you each a dollar, and you can grab a hamburger and shake for lunch at the soda shop too."

A dollar? Constance thought. That wouldn't be nearly enough to buy what they needed. A hamburger itself costs more than that. *Poor Aunt Sylvi. She must not have much money.* "Thank you," she said politely. "But it's okay. I'm afraid a hamburger alone will cost almost two dollars."

"Two dollars?" Joseph cried out.

"Oh, dear me!" Aunt Sylvi gasped.

"Two whole dollars?" Joseph continued in disbelief. "For a *hamburger*?"

Constance sat stunned for a moment. She did not understand their reaction. It didn't occur to any of them that she was from nearly fifty years in the future.

Finally, Aunt Sylvi chuckled. "I see things get a little more expensive in the years to come. This is

1959, dear. You can buy a hamburger and a milk-shake for about thirty cents."

"What?" Constance was dumbfounded. "Thirty cents?"

"Two whole dollars?" Joseph repeated.

"Wow! That's crazy," Constance continued. "How much are candy bars?"

"About a nickel," Aunt Sylvi replied.

"A *nickel*? Wow! Let's see." Constance rested her chin on her hand and looked toward the ceiling. "If candy bars are five cents, how many can I get with my birthday money? Grandpa gave me twenty dollars."

"Twenty dollars?" Joseph nearly choked on his corn.

Aunt Sylvi spewed water from her mouth onto the table. "Goodness, child!" She wiped her face with a napkin. "You had better let me hold on to that money for you. And you can come to me if you need anything!"

"Okay, Aunt Sylvi." Constance smiled and shook her head. "That's just *craziness*!"

They all sat quietly for a moment. It suddenly was very clear that Constance *had* come from another time.

"How old would I be where you live, Connie?" Joseph inquired. He had completely stopped eating at this point.

"Well, how old are you now?" Constance asked.

"Twelve."

"I figured it up earlier. I traveled back forty-seven years. So forty-seven plus twelve equals . . ." They both thought for a moment.

"Sixty-one?" Joseph guessed.

Constance shook her head and counted on her fingers. "No, fifty-nine."

"Fifty-nine? Gee! How old are you, Aunt Sylvi?"

"Oh, goodness. I'm a little older than fifty-nine, but thanks all the same." She chuckled as she started to clear the dishes.

"That's just crazy," Constance repeated. "Just crazy!" She stared at Joseph and shook her head.

"I guess you'd better respect your elders!" Joseph teased and got up from the table. As he left, he wadded up his napkin and then threw it at her.

"Hey!" Constance laughed and tried to catch it. She promptly got up and began to carry the dishes to the sink.

"Got any dessert?" Joseph asked Aunt Sylvi as he set his dishes on the counter.

"As a matter of fact," she answered, "I made a surprise." Aunt Sylvi opened an upper cabinet, reached up high, and pulled out a tin of cookies.

"Snickerdoodles? Ah, Aunt Sylvi. You're the greatest!" Joseph gushed and gave her a big hug.

"But not until the dishes are cleared and washed!" She placed her hands on his shoulders and pointed him toward the dining room.

"All right," he sniped. "Connie, you wash and I'll dry."

Aunt Sylvi stacked the dishes by the sink as the two got started with their chores. She gathered the tablecloth and napkins and carried them off to the laundry. Over her shoulder she said, "You kids finish up here, and I'll go make up the bed for Connie. I'll put you in the room next to Joseph. Were you able to find some nightclothes in Marie's things, dear?" she asked sweetly.

"I sure did, thanks. I'm all set," Constance replied, still washing the dishes. Grandpa didn't have a dishwasher, so she was used to helping him wash and dry. *I guess I had better get used to washing the dishes now that I am going to live in his house. I wonder if I'll ever get back.* Her thoughts of home dwindled as Joseph began to talk about their day tomorrow.

"Hey, want to play Monopoly when we're done here?" he asked.

"You have Monopoly? Okay. Sure." She grabbed the last few pots and washed them in the soapy water.

When the last dish was dried and put away, Joseph brought in the game and set it on the kitchen table next to the snickerdoodles. "Who do you want to be?" His favorite was the hat, but she called it first and he didn't argue. He chose the car and rolled the dice to see who would go first. Constance rolled a five.

"Let's see you beat that!" she said smugly.

Joseph picked up the dice, pretended to spit on it a little, shook it in his hands, and let it roll. "Six! Ha! Would you like to see me do it again?"

"Play nice!" Aunt Sylvi scolded as she returned to the kitchen and began to gather ingredients needed to make the birthday cake for Constance. She grabbed the butter and eggs. Then she reached for the sugar and the flour, but the flour canister slipped from her fingers and tumbled to the floor. "Oh goodness me!" she cried. There was flour everywhere! In her apron pockets, in her shoes, even in her hair. She looked up at the two kids, and all three howled with laughter.

"You go get yourself cleaned up, and we'll tidy up in here," Constance suggested. She was eager to get a break from the game. Joseph was a brutal Monopoly player.

"Oh, thank you, dear." Aunt Sylvi giggled and left for her room. "Believe it or not, I did manage to get a little in the bowl!"

Joseph went to the back porch for the broom. He didn't really want to stop the game, but he did anyway. They cleaned up the flour from the countertop and the kitchen floor. Joseph even swept up the trail Aunt Sylvi had made on the way to her room. Suddenly, a large clap of thunder startled them both, and they scurried back to their game.

Aunt Sylvi returned in a fresh apron as the rain began to fall outside. She quickly mixed the ingredients for the cake, separated the batter into two pans, and popped them into the oven. She sat for a while as the cake baked and watched their Monopoly game. She reminded Joseph more than once that Connie was their guest and that maybe he could play a little nicer. "Winning isn't everything," she reminded him as she got up to check the cakes.

Once they were done, Aunt Sylvi pulled them from the oven and set them out to cool. She promptly whipped up some tempting chocolate frosting and left the bowl near the cakes. As she untied her apron she announced, "I'm going to take a quick bath. You keep those fingers of yours out of that frosting, Joseph Salvatore Gordano!" His name faded as she disappeared down the hall. Joseph raised an eyebrow and stared at Constance. The minute he heard the bath water running, a sneaky smile came over his face.

"Joseph!" Constance snapped. "You heard Aunt Sylvi!"

He raised both eyebrows, smiled even bigger, and darted toward the bowl. Before she knew it, he had a fingerful of frosting. "Mm hm!" Joseph exclaimed and stuck it in his mouth.

"I cannot believe you just did that!" Constance leaned forward to check down the hall.

"You want some, don't you?" he asked with his index finger still in the air.

Constance giggled. "Okay, maybe just a little." She ran to the bowl to get herself a taste. As she tasted it her eyes grew wide, and she looked at Joseph in disbelief.

"See what I mean?" He nodded in agreement. Suddenly, a noise came from the hallway, and they both scrambled back to their seats.

Aunt Sylvi returned with her apron over her housecoat. "Dear me," she said without expression as she looked in the bowl. "It seems we have some mice in the house." She looked slowly over her shoulder. Neither Constance nor Joseph could keep a straight face.

"I am so sorry, Aunt Sylvi." Constance tried not to smile. "It was totally *his* fault."

"Thanks a lot!" He smirked back. "Some friend you are!"

They both laughed and returned to their game. Without looking up, Constance quietly said, "By the way, it's really yummy."

"Thank you," Aunt Sylvi replied warmly. "I remember when Joseph's father was young, he couldn't keep his fingers out of the frosting either."

It rained hard as she frosted the cake and cleaned up her dishes. Soon, Joseph bought Constance's last few properties, and everyone was ready to call it a night. Aunt Sylvi took her upstairs to show her where everything was for the bath. Aunt Sylvi turned on the water and poured in what she said was her best lavender bubble bath. "Soak as long as you like, dear. You've earned it today." She pulled the door closed.

The water felt great as Constance slipped into the tub. It was so warm and it smelled so good. In her mind, the day was like a one-hundred-piece puzzle and she couldn't find the corner pieces. How could this be happening? Wasn't it just this morning that her parents had left for Italy? She wondered if Anthony even realized she was gone. For a moment she felt homesick, but then she thought of the plan Joseph had to get her back, and she felt somewhat reassured.

As the water began to cool, she pulled the plug with her toes and grabbed her towel. She wrapped it around her head and put on one of Marie's nightgowns. As she buttoned it up, it occurred to her how much she really hated Monopoly. *No way am I playing with him again tomorrow.*

While Constance took her bath, Joseph picked up all the game pieces and money and stashed the box under his bed. He took a quick shower downstairs and recalled the moment she fell into the closet. It was the strangest thing he had ever seen. He was excited about tomorrow and was certain he could get her home, although he really liked having her around. As he toweled off and dressed for bed, it occurred to him how much he really loved Monopoly. *I can't wait to play again tomorrow!*

Soon, Aunt Sylvi had tucked everyone snugly into their beds. "How are you, dear?" she asked Constance as she sat down beside her and folded her sheet over the top of the blanket.

"I'm okay, I guess." Secretly, she missed her mom and dad. At home, her mom would lie down beside Constance, and they would take turns making up stories. Sometimes, she would ask her mom to tell the story of how she and her dad met, or the day she was born, or how Anthony read her bedtime stories when she was a baby.

Aunt Sylvi could sense how Constance felt. "Don't you worry, dear. We'll figure this out. I always talk to God when I don't know what to do, and an answer always comes. Even if it's not right away."

Constance smiled. "You sound like my dad."

"Well, he must be a very smart man," Aunt Sylvi replied. "Now, rest up. We have a lot to do tomorrow." She got up from the bed and smoothed the blankets with her hands.

As she started to leave, Constance quietly asked, "Aunt Sylvi? Can I please give you a hug?"

"Of course you may, dear. I can't think of anything I would like more." She sat back down and hugged Constance gently, then stayed seated until she had settled herself under the covers. "I'll see you in the morning," Aunt Sylvi said, placing her hand on the side of Constance's head.

Aunt Sylvi stood and turned out the light. As she pulled the door closed, she said one last time, "I'll see you in the morning." The thunder boomed as she went downstairs to lock up the house and go to bed. She sat on the end of her bed to remove her slippers and leaned over to set them on the floor. "Oh goodness," she mumbled and noticed even more flour on the floor near her dresser. "It will have to wait until morning." She snuggled into bed and turned off the lamp. *What a day!*

Upstairs, Constance had finished her prayers when she noticed that Aunt Sylvi's sheets were softer than any sheets they had at her own house. Why was that? How did she get them so soft? Different laundry soap? Fabric softener? Did they even *have* fabric softener? She closed her eyes and moved her legs around. She would have to talk to her mom about this when she got home.

Constance listened to the storm outside. The wind was loud and made eerie noises against the windows. She was sometimes scared of thunderstorms, and the lightning did seem a bit too close to this unfamiliar house. She closed her eyes and tried to relax. If she were home right now, her mom would be snuggled up beside her, probably extra close because of the storm. She would be telling the "How Mom and Daddy Met" story and getting to the part where her dad left a bag of groceries behind at the market, and her mom picked it up accidentally with her bags. When her mom got it home, she discovered it contained Fig Newtons, canned asparagus—both items her mom could not stand—men's shaving lotion, and her dad's wallet.

Her mom found his address on his driver's license and took it back to him. They ended up talking in the doorway for nearly an hour because her mom refused to go into his apartment. She informed him that she never entered strange men's homes. He told her he was offended. That he wasn't *that* strange! Then they laughed and she tried to explain that she meant "strangers."

Just as Constance was about to get to the part where her dad asked her mom out on their first date, she heard a soft tapping at the door. It was Joseph.

"Aunt Sylvi said I could sleep on your floor if you were scared." He peeked into the room.

"Sure. Thanks," Constance said with a smile. Truth was, she *was* a little spooked. The story of how her mom and dad met wasn't working to relax her this time. Maybe it wasn't the same if her mom didn't tell it. The wind and thunder sounded just awful outside.

"No problem," Joseph whispered. "I'll be right back!" He returned with his sleeping bag and unrolled it beside her bed. They both lay there and listened to the storm. The lightning danced across the walls. Neither could quit thinking about their day, and each other.

"Joseph," Constance whispered.

"Yeah, Connie?" He rolled over to face her.

"I'm kinda glad I fell through your closet."

"Me too," Joseph said.

"Crazy day, huh?" she muttered as they drifted off to sleep.

CHAPTER 4

The Break-In

Voices and footsteps woke Constance. She remained still for a moment with her eyes closed. She wasn't quite ready to wake up. *What is all that noise downstairs?* Did her brother have friends over this early? *Wait a minute!* Her eyes popped open. She wasn't at home. She was still at Aunt Sylvi's house, fifty years back in time! She leaned over to find Joseph sound asleep on the floor. She laid back down and took a deep breath. It wasn't a dream.

The noises downstairs were getting louder. Men shouted back and forth, and sounds of people were all about. "Joseph." She poked at him with her toe. "Joseph. Wake up!" He didn't move. She kicked him in the rear end. "Joseph! Get up! Something's going on downstairs!"

"Huh? What? What happened?" He sat straight up in his sleeping bag.

His reaction made Constance laugh. "Something's going on downstairs," she repeated.

"What?" He looked over at her. Suddenly, he was alarmed by the noises. "Who is that?" They both jumped up and ran down the hallway. They stopped at the top of the long staircase where they could see the activity below.

Two police officers moved about in the entryway, and a large, gray-haired man in a suit sat at the kitchen table. They assumed he was talking to Aunt Sylvi, but they couldn't see her. Finally, she came to the kitchen table with two coffee cups; one for the man in the suit and one for herself. The man dunked a cookie into his coffee as he talked with Aunt Sylvi. He wrote notes in a small notebook.

Joseph gasped! "He's eating our snickerdoodles!"

"Will you stop!" Constance said and slugged him in the arm. "Something's going on!"

"Say there ... Aunt Sylvi's crying!" Joseph scowled and became serious. "You stay here." He ran down the steps and raced to his aunt's side. "Aunt Sylvi!" he cried as he entered the kitchen. "Are you all right? What's going on?" With his arm around her shoulder, he turned to the strange man at the table.

"Things will be fine, son," the officer said and extended his card to Joseph. "Michael Rafferty, Detective. Seventeenth Precinct. I'm afraid there has been a break-in."

"All my jewelry is gone." Aunt Sylvi sobbed into her handkerchief. "Everything. My diamonds from your Uncle Sal, God rest his soul. Your great-grand-mother's pearls. Everything."

"What?" Joseph questioned. "How?"

"Broke in through the back door," Detective Rafferty explained.

Joseph heard Constance gasp at the top of the stairs. He looked up at her. Their eyes met. She held her hands over her mouth in disbelief. She turned and hurried back into the bedroom. Joseph wanted to go check on her, but he couldn't leave Aunt Sylvi.

In the bedroom, Constance quickly made up her bed and threw on one of Marie's outfits. She, too, felt like she needed to be with Aunt Sylvi. She wanted to know more about what had happened. She opened the door and ran down the hall. Quickly, she walked down the long staircase and saw that Detective Rafferty, Aunt Sylvi, and Joseph had moved to the front entryway. She hesitated.

"My boys will be finished here within the hour. Someone will be by to fix the back door later today. And remember, we have a pretty good idea who did this. They knew what they were doing, but we don't feel like you and your family are in any danger," Detective Rafferty explained. "However, just to be sure you feel safe, I am stepping up the patrols in your area."

"Thank you, Detective," Aunt Sylvi said. "And I'll be sure to call you if I think of anything that might be of help to the investigation."

"You call me, too, son, if you see anything suspicious," Detective Rafferty said to Joseph.

"Yes, sir, Detective. I will." He closed the door when the man left. "Let's go sit back down, Aunt Sylvi." Constance ran to join them.

Aunt Sylvi sat down at the kitchen table and blew her nose into her hanky. "This is terrible," Constance whispered to Joseph.

"We'll be okay, dear," Aunt Sylvi bravely reassured her as she wiped her eyes. "No one was hurt. We are all safe. They were just *things*." But she was once again overcome with sobs. Both Constance and Joseph tried to comfort her. They held her tight and stroked her back. A knock at the front door interrupted them.

"I'll get it," Joseph said. "It's probably one of the patrolmen."

"Dear! You are still in your nightclothes. Go up and get dressed. Connie and I will get the door."

Joseph agreed and took the stairs two at a time as Aunt Sylvi and Constance answered the door. It wasn't a policeman after all. It was a girl about her age and a lady.

"Oh, do come in," Aunt Sylvi said as she opened the door. "Connie, this is Katherine Rose O'Malley and her mother, Caroline. They live across the street. This is our dear friend, Connie . . . I mean *Constance*. Won't you sit down?" She motioned to a parlor area across the hall from the dining room.

"What's happened, Sylvi?" Mrs. O'Malley asked. "What's all the commotion about?" Aunt Sylvi held back her tears and explained the situation. As she heard it all again, Constance got the chills.

Joseph bounded into the room. "Who was it?" He stopped abruptly when he saw Katherine and her mother. "Oh, hello Katherine Rose," he murmured and looked at the floor. He sat down beside Constance on a small sofa.

"Hello," Katherine answered shyly. Joseph began to fidget. He fiddled with a string that hung from his shorts. Constance looked up at Katherine Rose, then back at Joseph. Was this the same friend who was playing Cowboys and Indians yesterday in the closet? The same friend who talked almost as much as she did? She gave Joseph an elbow to the side. He quickly returned the favor but with a lot more force. Constance winced and grabbed her ribs.

"Would you please say hello to Katherine's mother, Joseph?" Aunt Sylvi prodded.

"Yes, ma'am. I'm sorry. Good morning, Mrs. O'Malley."

"Good morning, Joseph," Mrs. O'Malley replied, and smiled at Aunt Sylvi. "Will you all be all right here?"

"Oh yes, thank you," Aunt Sylvi answered. "Detective Rafferty is the dearest man. He assured us there was nothing to be afraid of and said the patrolmen would watch the house."

As Aunt Sylvi and Mrs. O'Malley talked, Joseph and Katherine stole glances at one another. *Oh, brother!* Constance thought. *This is embarrassing!*

Before long, Katherine and her mother turned to leave. "Can we ask them over for cake, Aunt Sylvi? Can we?" Joseph pleaded.

"Why certainly. That's a fine idea!" Aunt Sylvi turned to explain to Mrs. O'Malley. "Constance has recently turned eleven, and we missed her birthday. I have a gorgeous chocolate cake in the kitchen that we plan to eat after dinner. Can you join us this evening? It will be a true party!"

Katherine's face lit up. She turned to her mother for an answer. "I'm sorry, sweetheart." She looked down at her daughter. "Thank you anyway, Sylvi. We're going to visit Katherine's grandmother tonight. We'll be sure to come by later in the week." Both Katherine and Joseph looked terribly sad. They said goodbye and Joseph closed the door behind them.

"So, how long have you been in L-O-V-E with Katherine Rose O'Malley?" Constance teased.

"Aw, cut it out!" Joseph said and shoved her from behind. She just laughed.

"All right, you two!" Aunt Sylvi interrupted. "Let's go make ourselves some pancakes. I understand they are a favorite of yours, Constance."

She smiled at Joseph. "They are! For sure! Thank you."

Into the kitchen they went, where they all three did their part to prepare breakfast. Aunt Sylvi made the pancakes, Joseph set the table, and Constance cut up some oranges and bananas.

"We have a very busy day today," Aunt Sylvi said as she sat down at the kitchen table. "Joseph?" He smiled at her and said a quick blessing before he passed around the pancakes. "I'm going to call the library as soon as we've finished eating. I'm going to ask that nice young man behind the counter . . . What's his name?"

"Thomas," Joseph answered.

"Yes, Thomas. I'm going to call Thomas and ask him to pull all the books he can find on time travel. He's sure to think I've completely lost my marbles!" She chuckled and swirled a bite of banana in her pancake syrup.

"That sounds great," Constance said.

"We're going to take the bikes up to the dime store and get our supplies. And don't forget! You said we could have a hamburger at the soda shop," Joseph reminded Aunt Sylvi. "Where are the bicycles?"

"In the garage, dear. But Marie hasn't had them out yet, so you'll need to clean them up. There are some old rags out there in a tub. You'll see them. And do try to keep an eye on the time. With all that has gone on, I'd rather you not be out all day."

"Sure, Aunt Sylvi, no problem." Joseph got up from the table and kissed his aunt on the cheek. "Thanks for breakfast."

Constance took her dishes to the sink. "Do you need some help cleaning up?"

"No, dear. Thank you." Aunt Sylvi dismissed them with a wave. "You two run along. This won't take but a minute."

"Okay, thanks." Connie followed Joseph from the room. "The pancakes were wonderful." But her dad's would always be her favorite.

"Want us to wait until you're ready to go?" Joseph looked back into the kitchen. "Will you be okay alone?"

Aunt Sylvi laughed. "I'm not alone, dear. There are three patrolmen out back. I'll be fine." She reached into her apron pocket and pulled out two one-dollar bills. "You almost forgot your money!"

"Oh yeah! Thanks!" He ran back, kissed her on the cheek again, and grabbed the money.

A glass pane in the door had been broken. Although most of the glass had been cleaned up, there was still a crunching sound under their feet as they made their way to the back porch. For a moment, Constance questioned how no one had heard the glass breaking, but then she remembered the storm.

Aunt Sylvi was right. There were three policemen on the stoop who were talking and writing in small notebooks like Rafferty's. As she and Joseph passed, one lifted his head and said, "Hey, kid," to Joseph. Another smiled at Constance, and the third didn't look up at all.

"Who do you think did this?" Joseph asked.

Detective Rafferty said they had a good idea. He said whoever did it "knew what they were doing."

Did that mean they knew how to break into a house? Or did that mean they knew what jewels Aunt Sylvi had and where she kept them? Who could know all that?

"Hey, Joseph." She followed him behind the house to the garage. "Did your Aunt Sylvi ever wear her jewelry?"

"Sometimes to church," he said and walked across the gravel driveway. "But that's about it."

"Hm, I wonder if it could be someone from her church. Surely not though," Constance mumbled and then shook her head.

"What?" Joseph asked.

"Nothing," Constance answered, then followed him through the side door. The garage smelled like the old shed where Grandpa kept his tractor. *Motor oil*, she thought. It made her smile. She looked around. It was a lot bigger inside than she expected. To the left was a long workbench covered with tools, a few small pieces of rock, and some kind of chalky dust. "What's all this?" She picked up a small pebble.

"I don't know. Seems like it fell from the ceiling." Joseph looked up, only to discover wooden rafters. "That's weird. Hey! Look at this!" he cried, unconcerned with the rock mess. There was a large motorcycle parked alongside the workbench. "It's my Uncle Gordy's. Isn't it great?" He stroked the leather seat as he passed. "Last summer Gordy took me on a long motorcycle ride down to the river. It was super."

On the far side of the garage was a huge yellow car with white seats. Constance had never seen a car quite that big. The bikes were hanging from hooks on the back wall about halfway between the car and the motorcycle. They were big too. They reminded her of the bikes from *The Sound of Music.*

"I think those are the rags Aunt Sylvi was talking about. If you want to grab a couple, I'll get the bikes down," Joseph directed.

Constance evaluated her choices, decided on two soft blue towels, and removed them from the tub. When she turned around, the bikes were already off the wall and propped up on their kickstands.

"Wow! That was fast!"

"Well, I am an exceptional specimen of a man!" Joseph teased. He took one of the rags from Constance and cleaned off the black bike. "You can have the red one."

After they shined up the bikes, they returned the rags to the bucket. Joseph maneuvered around the motorcycle and began to leave the garage.

"What about helmets?" Constance questioned.

"What do you mean?" Joseph asked.

"We need bike helmets."

"We're not riding the motorcycle; we're riding the bicycles."

"Do you know how many people are injured each year because they didn't wear a helmet?" Constance continued.

"You have *got* to be kidding me." Joseph sighed and parked his bike. He walked over to the motor-cycle and removed Uncle Gordy's motorcycle helmet. "You want a helmet? Here's a helmet!" He plopped it on her head and walked away.

"This is crazy!" Constance muttered while trying to adjust the chin strap. "I cannot believe you don't wear bicycle helmets."

"Nobody does, Connie. I've never even heard of such a thing!"

Determined to wear the wobbly, too-large helmet, Constance walked out of the garage. Every time she reached for her handlebars, the helmet slid down over her eyes. Finally, with her head cocked back and slightly to the left, she stiffly walked her bike through the grass to the back gate. She contem-plated her next move. How would she get on the bike without the humongous helmet slipping again? "Oh, forget it!" she said frustratedly and called ahead to Joseph, "Hang on!" She leaned her bike against the fence and ran back to the garage. As she took off the helmet, she noticed that the wall behind the workbench was made of cement blocks that were painted white. *That must be where all this dust came from*, she thought, scanning the wall. She saw lots of cracks but no real holes. *Interesting.* She thought for a moment and then ran back to her bike and Joseph.

"Thank goodness!" Joseph said and hopped on his bike. "You looked ridiculous."

CHAPTER 5

Freedom

It was a great day for a bike ride. The sun was hot, but the breeze was cool. To Connie, it seemed as if she were riding through a movie. Everything looked different somehow. She caught herself staring at everyone she passed. The hairstyles. The clothes. Everyone looked like they had stepped out of the pictures from her grandpa's photo album. And the cars were huge!

"I can't believe how different everything looks," she told Joseph. They rode side by side down the middle of the street.

"Really? How so?"

"It's hard to explain. Let's just say cars and hair both get smaller."

Joseph chuckled. He stood up on his pedals and yelled, "Let's race!" He took off in a flash. Constance quickly followed, but it was hard to maneuver such a large bicycle. She had almost caught up with him when he threw his hands in the air and screamed, "The champion!"

They continued to ride in silence for a short time. Constance smiled the entire trip. She loved the houses. Some had larger yards with small white fences; others boasted beautiful flowers.

Finally, they began to pass fewer houses and more small shops. Connie could not believe how many kids there were walking around, riding bikes, and sitting on park benches. *Where are their parents?* she wondered. Her mom and dad had always said, "When I was young, we didn't have to worry about the stuff kids worry about today." And, "I would leave the house in the morning on my bicycle and not return until dinner time." This must be what they were talking about. It felt good to not have a parent constantly around. She liked the independence. She felt free. She felt older.

Joseph pointed out the soda shop where they would have lunch. It was packed with kids and teenagers. Just up the street was the dime store. She smiled as the wind blew in her face. She let the breeze carry her hair as they pedaled the rest of the way.

Joseph parked his bike by the front door of the dime store, and Connie did the same. At first she was surprised when they parked the bikes without locks on them. But then she realized there were a lot of things that were going to surprise her that day, including the short, round man with a ring of black hair who greeted them as they entered the store.

"Good morning there, young people! What can I get for you this fine day?"

"Hello, Mr. McGillicutty. Today we need everything you've got to start a detective agency," Joseph explained.

"Detectives, huh? That *is* a tall order. Let me see what we have over in our 'spy' section." He winked and led them through the store. "We have the 'Super Spy Deluxe' here. It comes with a finger printing kit, magnifying glasses, invisible ink, instructions, and a special listening device."

"Wow! How much is it?" Joseph asked, mesmerized by the possibility of owning such a prize.

"Looks like it is marked two dollars," Mr. McGillicutty replied.

"Oh." Joseph sighed disappointedly. "We only have two dollars between us. We still need to buy paint to make a sign and get lunch up at the soda shop."

"Well, then I have just the thing. How about a super-powerful magnifying glass? Comes with a handy travel case. They are fifteen cents each. Plus, I can throw in some 'evidence' bags up at the front counter."

"Gee, that sounds swell!" Joseph forgot how he had yearned for the "Super Spy Deluxe."

"And I have just the right paint for your sign." Mr. McGillicutty led them to an aisle full of school and art supplies.

Connie grabbed some purple paint, and Joseph grabbed some red. They found a roll of brown paper and were off. As promised, Mr. McGillicutty threw in some small brown bags and offered them each a licorice whip. They stashed their supplies and candy in her empty backpack and climbed on their bikes.

"Where to now?" Connie asked. She sneaked a bite of licorice before she threw her backpack over her shoulder.

"I'm kinda hungry." Joseph grimaced and rubbed his hand over his stomach. "Let's get lunch!" He paused to look for cars and launched into the street. Connie hurried to catch up.

"Sure, uh, that sounds great." She tried to watch for cars. "Wait up!" Before she knew it, they were in front of the soda shop where the sidewalk was crowded with parked bicycles.

"Down here!" Joseph pointed around the corner. They propped their bikes against a brick wall in a narrow alley. "Let's go!" Joseph grabbed her hand, dashed around the corner, and ducked through the front door just as someone was leaving. He looked around and promptly pulled Connie toward a booth by the window.

She smiled as she plopped down on the red vinyl seat. "This is awesome!" she exclaimed. She did not want to forget one moment of this. She listened to the music that someone had selected. It sounded like the music her dad listened to in the car. She noticed some kids huddled around the jukebox. Two girls stood next to it and danced. A bunch of boys sat on stools up at the front counter. "This place is great!" She looked at the red-and-white checkered floor.

Suddenly, a woman with big yellow hair was standing at their table. "Hiya, kids!" She snapped the pink bubble gum she was chewing. "What's it gonna be?"

"I'll have a hamburger, some French fries, and an extra-thick chocolate shake," Joseph declared hungrily.

The waitress pulled a pencil from her hair and wrote his order down on a small pad. "And for you, doll?" She turned to look at Connie.

"I'll have the same," she replied. "Thank you." The waitress's nametag said "Donna Sue," and something about her seemed glamorous.

"This is crazy," Connie said once the waitress had left. "It is all so hard to understand."

Joseph looked at her with concern. "I'm sorry, Connie. We'll get you home so—"

He was cut off by someone yelling, "Hey, Gordano! You made it!" Two boys approached their table. "I thought you were coming by yesterday," one of them said. Quickly, he noticed Connie. "I'm Sonny," he said gently.

She could feel her face get warm. He was very cute. Before she could respond, Joseph said, "Fellas, this is Connie, or Constance. I call her Connie though. She's . . . a friend of the family. Connie, these are my pals, Sonny and Pete. Have a seat. We just ordered."

"Hi!" Pete smiled as he sat beside Joseph. "Get a load of this!" He unstrapped something from around his neck. It was a long, narrow box, bigger than Pete's hand. He fiddled with it a second and it popped open. It was a camera. "Smile!" He pointed it at Joseph and took his picture.

"Gee, that's swell!" Joseph agreed. He watched Pete pull something from the camera. "What is that?"

"That's the picture!" Sonny explained. "You can wait and watch it develop! Isn't that terrific?"

"Where did you get that?" Joseph was amazed.

"His Uncle Jim." Sonny was so excited about Pete's new gadget; he couldn't wait to share in his news.

"You remember him!" Pete broke in. "He's the one who travels all the time. He sends me film and everything. My mom thinks it's too extravagant, but I don't think so."

"Me neither!" Joseph agreed.

The boys continued to discuss the camera, and Pete sat beside Joseph, which left Connie nervous about sitting beside Sonny.

Oh no! she thought. *The cute one is sitting beside me!* What was wrong with her? No boy had ever made her feel like this before. She had tons of boys back home who were her friends, but she never felt weird about any of them. *Do I look okay?* Who was she kidding? She looked like a dork wearing "Cousin Marie's" stripes. She wished she at least had her lip gloss on hand.

As Sonny sat down, his arm brushed against hers and she quickly pulled away. *Okay, Constance, he's just a stupid boy! Pull it together!*

"Pete's been taking pictures all over town!" Sonny announced.

"May I see your picture of Joseph?" Connie asked. Pete slid it across the table.

"You fellas are not going to believe it, but somebody broke into Aunt Sylvi's house last night and stole all her jewelry," Joseph informed the guys.

"No kidding?" Pete gasped. He took a picture of Connie looking at the picture of Joseph.

"Is she okay?" Sonny asked.

"She's fine," Joseph answered, "just a little shook up."

Donna Sue with the yellow hair returned with a tray of food. "You boys ordering?" she asked as she sat Joseph and Connie's plates and shakes in front of them.

"Sure! I'll have what they are having," Sonny answered.

"Let's see . . . How about a double cheeseburger with onion rings and a strawberry malted?" Pete asked.

"You got it, sugar," Donna Sue said and returned her pencil to her hair.

"So, Connie, where are you from? And how long are you staying?" Sonny asked. He turned slightly in his seat to see her better. Pete took their picture.

Connie looked at Pete. "Oh, I'm f-from P-Pittsburg, Kansas," she stuttered. She was caught off guard by the picture and the question. She looked over at Joseph and said, "And I'm . . . um . . . not really certain how long I'm staying. It's hard to say."

"Well, if you are here tomorrow night, what do you say we all go to the carnival together?" Sonny suggested.

"That sounds swell!" Pete exclaimed. "They get in town tomorrow morning to set up. Think of the photos!"

"Connie, will you come?" Sonny asked.

"Oh, uh . . . well, sure. I'm sure that will be okay. Right, Joseph? I mean, we don't know for *sure* if I'll be here, but if I am—"

"We'll be there," Joseph interrupted. He looked at Connie and smiled. He opened his eye as wide as he could and looked over at Sonny, then back at Connie, then over to Sonny, and then back at Connie, until Connie finally kicked him under the table.

"Ouch!" Joseph squealed. Connie smiled.

Pete and Sonny's food arrived, and the friends sat and talked about what they had been doing since Joseph's last visit. Connie learned that Pete and Sonny both lived in Aunt Sylvi's neighborhood, and every summer they looked forward to Joseph's visits. They met him one day while they were out playing stick ball in the street and had become the best of friends.

According to Pete, the most exciting thing that had happened to him since last summer was his Uncle Jim's visit. Uncle Jim had been in Africa and told Pete and his little brothers stories of lions, zebras, and small men in tribes who carried spears. He had pictures of them all. Pete was extremely impressed. He told of when Uncle Jim gave him the camera. Pete could hardly believe it, but his mother almost didn't let him keep it. Sonny laughed and told Joseph, "Pete says that having the camera has changed his entire outlook on life!" Sonny and Joseph laughed.

So did Connie who said, "It sounds like he's been watching *Save My Life Suzie.* The laughter died abruptly, and all three boys looked at her.

"What?" Joseph asked with raised eyebrows.

"Oh, nothing," Connie said. "Just a show we watch back home." *Save My Life Suzie? What was I thinking?* She wished she could just crawl under the table. She promptly changed the subject. "Sonny, what have you been up to since you last saw Joseph?"

"Oh, nothing too exciting for me!" Sonny laughed. "Just the same old after-school job helping my uncle." He looked across the table at his friends and they all smiled.

"What? What is it?" Connie looked at them, wondering what the big secret was.

"I usually tell all kinds of stories to the fellas, but I don't think I'd better today. Especially since we're eating, and with a lady present."

"Ah, come on, Sonny. Just one little story? Connie doesn't count!" Joseph begged.

"Gordano! Come on!" Pete scolded him and glanced over at Connie.

"I don't count? That's nice. What's going on?" Connie was beginning to feel uncomfortable, and she didn't appreciate Joseph's comment.

"My uncle owns a meat packing plant. I generally have some pretty bloody tales. I'm sorry about that, Connie," Sonny explained. Then he turned to Joseph. "I think you owe her an apology!"

"He's right. I apologize, Connie. Really." Joseph looked at her. She could tell he was embarrassed.

"You're forgiven." Constance smiled at him.

"Listen, Petie." Sonny tossed his napkin on his plate. "We have to go. I promised my mom that I wouldn't be late for my doctor visit."

"Oh yeah!" Pete chuckled. "I forgot. Our boy here might have to get glasses!"

"Really? You poor thing," Joseph teased.

"What?" Connie quickly interrupted. "I think you would look very nice in glasses, Sonny."

"Really?" Sonny seemed pleased. "Then I'll be sure to ask for them whether I need them or not." He scooted out of the booth. "We will see you guys tomorrow. Connie, it was a pleasure."

"Yeah, nice meeting you, Connie," Pete said. "We will catch up with you later, Gordano."

"Goodbye. It was nice meeting you both." Connie blushed.

"See you later." Joseph nodded. As the boys left, a big grin came across his face. "Ooh, I think you would look *nice* in glasses, Sonny," he mimicked.

"Stop it!" Connie snapped.

"It was nice meeting you both, especially you, *Sonny*," he continued.

"Will you please stop it? You know, it really stinks! The first boy that I ever liked turns out to be someone born fifty years before me."

Joseph gasped. "I didn't think about it that way! Poor Sonny. He really looked sweet on you too! We have to tell him, you know?"

They were interrupted by the sound of gum popping. "You kids going to need anything else?" Donna Sue asked.

"No thanks." Joseph handed her their money, and she counted back his change. As they rose to leave, he said, "You know, I was thinking . . . What do you say we go up to the precinct and tell Detective Rafferty about how you got here? He is a real detective, and he might have some ideas."

"Or he'll think we are completely nuts." Connie sighed. "But it's worth a try, I guess."

The detective's card was in Joseph's pocket. He pulled it out and asked a man at the counter for directions to the address.

"Looks like it isn't far at all," Joseph said. "Let's go."

Connie thanked the man and followed Joseph out the door.

"We can go by the filling station where Uncle Gordy works. It's just up the road." Joseph hopped on his bike.

"Okay," Connie answered and then looked up at the sky. "Do you think it's going to rain?" The air felt like it was changing, and the sun was slowly being blocked by heavy gray clouds.

"I don't know. Why? Scared of a little rain?"

"I guess not," Connie said, shrugging her shoulders. *Thunder and lightning? Now that is another story*, she thought.

"Up here!" Joseph crossed to the other side of the street.

Connie could see that Joseph was headed to a gas station. *Aha!* she thought. *A filling station is a gas station. I get it now!* The gas pumps looked shiny and new, yet they also looked so old-fashioned compared to the ones they had in Pittsburg. At home, her mom or dad always pumped their own gas, but here there was a man doing it. He seemed very busy. He was washing the windshield and doing something under the hood as well. He wore the same blue jumpsuit Gordy wore.

"Hiya, Tony. My Uncle Gordy around?" Joseph asked.

Tony wiped his hands on a red rag and then shook his head. "Sorry, Joey. Gordy said he needed a few hours to take care of some business. He took off about a half hour ago."

Joseph thanked him and turned to Connie, "Detective Rafferty's office should be right around the corner."

He stopped briefly to look for cars, then zoomed across the street, made a quick turn, and almost tipped his bike.

"Nice moves!" Connie yelled. This neighborhood resembled Aunt Sylvi's more than the one by the diner. The tall brick houses were built closely together. There were some stores and restaurants scattered around, but it was hard to tell which were houses and which were stores.

At an intersection, Connie saw Uncle Gordy come out of a shop down the street. Over the door hung a sign that looked like a big watch. "Hey, isn't that Gordy right there?" she asked, pointing him out to Joseph.

Joseph stopped. "That's the jewelry store old man Smithers owns. I wonder what Uncle Gordy is doing in there."

"Maybe he's buying something for your Aunt Sylvi as a surprise since all of her stuff was stolen."

"Say, I bet you're right. That's just the kind of thing Uncle Gordy would do!" Joseph began to pedal again.

Before they knew it, they were standing in front of the Seventeenth Precinct. As they parked their bikes, Connie asked, "Are you sure we should tell Detective Rafferty about me and my time travel? He might think we are making up stories or something."

"What's he going to do? Throw us in the slammer? Come on!"

Connie shook her head. "This is absolutely crazy. Okay, let's go."

Inside the door were some wide wooden stairs. They began to climb the steps when they heard Detective Rafferty's voice. "It has to be the son, Vincent Gordano," Rafferty said. Connie and Joseph froze in their tracks. Rafferty continued, "We have seen him with the Barcolli brothers, and they are bad news. My guess is he's somehow over his head with gambling debts and he owes them money."

Joseph and Connie looked at each other in disbelief.

"Boys, we need to keep an eye on him. It should not take long to nail him down. He is not a criminal, just a desperate man who has gotten himself into a bad situation. My guess is he will lead us right to the stolen jewelry."

Detective Rafferty stopped talking. They heard footsteps coming toward them. Connie gasped. She looked at Joseph with wide eyes. Without a word, he grabbed her hand, and they turned and ran as fast as they could from the building. She struggled to stay on her feet. With one swift motion, Joseph jumped on his bike and pedaled furiously. Connie had trouble with her bike chain. When she was finally on the move, she cried out for Joseph to wait for her, but he continued to speed away.

She watched him turn the corner, and she knew he had taken it too fast. "Joseph!" she cried as his bike flew out from under him. His hands and face hit the pavement. "Oh my goodness! Oh my goodness!" She jumped from her moving bicycle and raced to him.

Joseph was bleeding from the chin and elbow, but he tried his best to fight back tears. He sat up and covered his face with his arm. "I can't believe this is happening. Rafferty is supposed to be one of the good guys. How could he possibly think that Uncle Gordy did this?" He pulled up the edge of his shirt and dabbed a little blood off his chin and stood up. "There is *no way* that Uncle Gordy stole from Aunt Sylvi. She's his *mother*. He would never do that." He looked at Connie, and then looked around. "Where's your bike?"

"Back there." She motioned with her head.

"Better go get it. Let's walk for a while," he suggested.

As Connie ran back to get her bike, she tried to process what had just happened. She wanted to believe that Gordy was innocent, but Joseph *did* say he had been acting weird. Maybe she and Joseph could somehow prove that Gordy *didn't* do it. *That is a great idea*, she thought. Proud of herself, she picked up her bike and walked it quickly back to Joseph.

"Listen, I have a crazy idea. Why don't we use the new Pentori and Gordano detective agency to prove that Gordy is innocent? We can try to figure out where he was when the break-in occurred, maybe even sneak into his room to search for clues!"

"Connie," Joseph exclaimed, "you are a genius! That is exactly what we will do. Prove that my uncle is innocent!"

"Great," she said. "I watch a lot of detective shows on the Mystery Channel! I know how to search for clues!"

"What do you mean, the 'Mystery Channel'?" Joseph looked puzzled.

"Never mind. But we need a plan," Connie said as they walked their bikes home.

They were nearly there when it started to sprinkle. They jumped back on their bikes and rode the rest of the way, determined to race the dark clouds that loomed overhead. Joseph went ahead and opened the garage door for Connie.

"Where do you think Gordy was last night?" she asked. She parked her bike next to the big yellow car. Joseph had already parked his there and was looking out the window at the rain. "Did he even come home after dinner?"

"I don't know," he replied. "It's really coming down out there now. I guess we can ask Aunt Sylvi. Surely she saw him this morning." He turned around and hoisted himself up on the workbench. Connie checked out the window and took a seat beside him. Once again, she noticed the white chalky dust scattered over the tools on the bench.

"In some shows I have seen," she explained, "they search a person's room to find clues that connect them to the crime. What if we search Gordy's room to find clues that prove he *didn't* commit the crime? Maybe we can find something that shows us where he was last night!"

"Another great idea, Detective Pentori." Joseph grinned. "We can wait until he leaves for work in the morning and look around without him even knowing." He turned around and peeked out the window. "Looks like the rain is letting up. Let's make a break for it."

Joseph jumped off the workbench and headed for the door. He stopped to wait for Connie. "Let's go!" he screamed. He put his head down and sprinted to the back porch. When she reached to open the door, she noticed the glass had been replaced.

Inside the entryway, Aunt Sylvi had laid down a towel. Joseph wiped his feet, removed his shoes, and placed them beside the door. Connie did the same.

"I cannot wait to eat my cake!" Connie rubbed her hands together. "That frosting is crazy good!"

"Aunt Sylvi, we're home!" Joseph announced, but there was no reply. "Aunt Sylvi?" he called again. No answer. Joseph looked at Connie. Something didn't feel right. Where was Aunt Sylvi?

"Aunt Sylvi!" Joseph called out in a panic.

"Aunt Sylvi! Where are you?" Connie cried out. Both were breathing deeper. Their hearts were pounding. Where was Aunt Sylvi?

"I'm in the dining room, dears," Aunt Sylvi finally answered. "What is all the fuss about?"

Joseph and Connie both let out heavy sighs. "Nothing, Aunt Sylvi." Joseph took another deep breath. "We just didn't see you there. Been to the library?" They entered the room to find Aunt Sylvi at the table, surrounded by books and papers.

"Yes, dears," she said disappointedly. "I've been to the library. But I am afraid most of the information I found is way over my head. Dear me, this Einstein fellow. Ooh!" Aunt Sylvi let out a giggle and tossed one of the papers in the air. "Time, space, relativity. Goodness me! I am afraid I am going to be of no help at all!"

Connie sighed. "I would give anything to get on the internet right now!"

"The what?" Joseph asked.

"Oh, forget it. Don't worry, Aunt Sylvi. I appreciate you trying."

"Child!" Aunt Sylvi reached over and took Joseph's face in her hand. "What have you done to your chin? We need to clean that up!"

"Naw, I'm all right." Joseph brushed her hand away. "Say, Aunt Sylvi"—Joseph pulled a chair out across from her and sat down—"what time did Uncle Gordy get home last night?"

"Sakes, I was fast asleep. I am not sure when he finally came in. He's usually not too late. Why do you ask?"

Joseph looked at Connie, who quickly explained, "We thought maybe he saw something when he came home. You know, something about the robbery."

Aunt Sylvi began to stack the papers she had strewn about. "He was long gone when I woke up this morning, love. I called him at work as soon as I realized what had happened. He said he had left through the front door and didn't notice there was anything wrong. He offered to come home, but I told him there was no reason. I had already telephoned the authorities. What about you, dears? Did you enjoy your day?"

"We sure did!" Connie smiled.

"Yeah, we got everything we needed up at the dime store and had lunch with Pete and Sonny at the malt shop."

"That's nice. How are they doing? Such fine young men." Aunt Sylvi nodded approvingly.

"Pete is just as crazy as ever. He has a new camera that his Uncle Jim gave him. It is something else! I predict he will drive us all mad with it by the end of the summer! Sonny may have to get glasses. Oh, and it looks like he is a little sweet on Connie."

"Oh dear!" Aunt Sylvi smiled and looked at Connie, whose face was a lovely shade of crimson. "Sonny is a dear boy. That is wonderful news."

"Aunt Sylvi," Joseph interjected, "Sonny is about fifty years older than Connie! It is terrible news! Poor fellow."

"Poor fellow? What about me?" Connie demanded. "I could really like this guy! Now I have to tell him I'm some freak from the future who fell through your closet!"

"You are not a freak, dear," Aunt Sylvi said soothingly. She gave Connie's hand a pat as she got up from the table. "You are just in a strange predicament. One that calls for snickerdoodles and milk."

"That's a swell idea!" Joseph followed Aunt Sylvi into the kitchen. "I am surprised there are any left the way you were feeding them to Rafferty this morning." He smiled and nudged his aunt.

"That is *Detective* Rafferty to you, young man!" Aunt Sylvi tried not to smile. "And it was the least I could do. He is doing everything he can to find who did this."

The jovial mood shifted to one that was much more serious. Connie and Joseph both thought of Rafferty's voice; he blamed Uncle Gordy. Joseph looked at Connie who gave him a half smile and shrugged her shoulders.

"Now, you two run along." Aunt Sylvi closed the tin of cookies after she put a few on a plate. "I have to get dinner started."

"What are we having?" Joseph called out on his way to the staircase. He carefully balanced the plate of cookies and a big glass of milk.

"Spaghetti and meatballs," Aunt Sylvi answered. "And birthday cake!"

"I cannot wait!" Connie shouted. She grabbed her backpack full of supplies and ran up the stairs behind Joseph. She just couldn't believe Aunt Sylvi had made her such a delicious looking cake. She felt like Aunt Sylvi was her aunt, too, and that Joseph had been her friend for years. *When did I get here?* she wondered. *Was it just yesterday?* It seemed like she had been there for days. Suddenly, in her daydreaming she realized she had almost spilled her milk. "Pay attention, Constance!" she said firmly. "Pay attention there, sister!" She made herself laugh.

Up in the attic, Joseph plopped down onto the plush sofa and placed the plate of cookies on a small table. Connie tossed her backpack onto the desk and grabbed a cookie. She slowly wandered over to one of the windows. It looked so dark outside, but it was still the afternoon. Grey clouds and rain had washed away the sunshine that had warmed them on their bike ride just hours ago.

Connie began to think of Sonny and of going home. It all seemed so crazy. How would she tell him? How would she get home? *When* would she get home? She gazed out the window and let her thoughts drift. Suddenly, something caught her eye. It was the car! The same car they had seen yesterday. The same two men who had yelled at Uncle Gordy. It was them! But this time they drove down the alley *behind* the house.

"Joseph! Joseph! It's them! They're back!" she screamed and watched the car slow down to a mere creep.

"What?" Joseph launched himself off the sofa and ran to the window.

"Do you think those are the Dragoli brothers?" Connie asked anxiously.

"*Barcolli* brothers," Joseph corrected. "And yes. I think that's who they are."

"They scare me! What do you think they are doing?"

"I don't know," Joseph admitted. His heart pounded so loudly; he was certain Connie could hear it.

Just as the car appeared to stop, it sped up again. The tires screeched as they turned back onto the street. Almost immediately, a police squad car turned down the alley.

"Whew!" Connie gasped. "Rafferty said they would add more men to patrol the area. They must have seen them."

They both made their way back to the sofa and chair where they collapsed. "You do realize that you will be sleeping on my floor again tonight," Connie said and bit into another cookie.

"You bet I am!" Joseph chuckled.

CHAPTER 6

Ol' Red

Connie and Joseph sat quietly with their snick-erdoodles and milk. They listened to the rain as it pinged off the metal gutters outside the window. "Do you have any brothers or sisters?" She realized she didn't really know much about him.

"Mmm." Joseph nodded with a mouthful of cookies. "A brother." He swallowed. "Dean. He's older. He works with my dad at the bank. That's what they do. Work at the bank."

"That's cool. What about your mom? What does she do?"

"What do you mean, 'What does she do?'" Joseph frowned.

"You know, like a job?" Connie couldn't believe he didn't understand.

"She takes care of us," Joseph answered with a shrug. "I guess that's her job."

"Oh, the poor woman! She probably deserves a raise!" Connie laughed and leaned up for another cookie. "By the way, your chin is bleeding again."

Joseph lifted the bottom of his shirt and once again dabbed the blood. He checked his elbow; it was fine. "I'll be back." He started down the stairs but quickly turned to grab one last cookie. "Try not to miss me too much."

"I'll do my best," Connie answered and pulled her feet into the chair.

The attic made a great clubhouse, but today it was a little dark and chilly. She watched the rain fall outside and followed the drops as they slid down the glass, thinking about the window over her bed at Grandpa's. It had been raining when she left. As she thought of her room at home, she drifted off to sleep.

Downstairs, Aunt Sylvi held Joseph firmly by the neck as she dabbed iodine on his scrape. "Blow! Blow! Blow!" he cried. "What is that stuff?"

"Goodness me!" Aunt Sylvi smiled. "The burn means it's working."

"Well, it's working all right!"

"Now," Aunt Sylvi continued, "you are going to need some of your Uncle Sal's special tape on that. You have split it wide open." She opened a drawer in the bathroom cabinet and pulled out a large roll of dark-yellow tape. She cut off a piece with small scissors and then cut it in half going the other direction. "All right now. Look up at me. Close your mouth, son. Chin up. Hold still, boy!" She steadied his face with her hand.

"Ouch! Aunt Sylvi!"

"You are almost done. Let me put a bandage over it and you will be good as new." She taped the bandage on, kissed his forehead, and cheerily said, "All set."

He took one last look in the mirror, thanked Aunt Sylvi, and headed back to the attic.

He hurried up the stairs and yelled, "Any cookies left, or did you eat them all?" His voice softened as he found Connie curled up, sound asleep.

Slightly disappointed, he turned and went back down to the kitchen. "Hey, Aunt Sylvi, where in the attic do you keep blankets and stuff?"

"In a cardboard box. I think it is over by the desk, dear." She didn't bother to turn around.

"Thanks!"

Upstairs, Joseph quietly found the box and pulled out a large patchwork quilt. Gently, he placed it over Connie and tucked it around her feet. He sat for a while and thought about how she fell into the closet and into another time. Was there some kind of trap door in the ceiling? Was there some super-cosmic tunnel that connected Aunt Sylvi's closet with hers? These questions both scared and inspired Joseph.

He left the attic and went to his bedroom. From his top dresser drawer, he pulled a small rubber ball he called "Ol' Red" and tucked it in his pocket. From the back porch he collected a broom and a step stool. Carefully, he carried these items up the stairs to the hall closet.

It was a large, square closet. He loved to play there. Aunt Sylvi used it mostly for hanging clothes, and there was generally nothing on the floor.

Joseph held the broom high over his head, and with the handle he began to thump the ceiling of the closet. *Thump! Thump! Thump!* He then took a step forward. *Thump! Thump! Thump!* He stepped forward again. *Thump! Thump! Thump!* The process continued until he had covered the entire surface of the ceiling. "Hm, no luck," he said. Time for plan B."

Up in the attic the thumping woke Connie. *Thump! Thump! Thump!* "What is that?" she said aloud. "Where is Joseph?" *Thump! Thump! Thump!* The mysterious sound beckoned her from the attic. Cautiously, she made her way down the hall.

Back in the closet Joseph prepared for plan B. He placed the step stool in the center of the closet and climbed to the third step. He took Ol' Red out of his pocket. She was a keen rubber ball. He had found her one day at the park by the climbing bars. She was red with small flecks of yellow and was the best bouncer Joseph had ever seen. However, at the moment, Joseph had forgotten that fact. He lifted her high over his head and threw her down with all his might. Like a rocket, Ol' Red bounced from the floor to the ceiling, to the floor, to the ceiling, to the floor, to ceiling, to floor, ceiling, floor, ceiling until she finally changed direction and started to bounce off the walls. Back and forth and back and forth. Joseph crouched down on the step stool and tucked in his head.

"Ahh!" he yelled.

At that moment Connie opened the closet door. Ol' Red ricocheted off the step stool, flew out the door, and barely missed her head. "Ahh!" she screamed and threw her hands in front of her face. "What in the world was that?" she asked as she looked over her shoulder.

Joseph chuckled and gave a heavy sigh. "That that was Ol' Red. She was plan B."

"Joseph Gordano! What is going on up there?" Aunt Sylvi cried from the bottom of the stairs.

"I'm sorry, Aunt Sylvi!" he called back. "I was just doing an experiment."

"Goodness me. I think it's time you came and experimented at setting the dinner table."

"Yes, ma'am," Joseph answered with a pout. He was disappointed that none of his experiments had worked.

"And bring my step stool and broom with you." Aunt Sylvi walked back into the kitchen. "Goodness, child."

"I'm not sure I understand the plan," Connie said. She retrieved the broom and took a good look in the closet. "But I do appreciate the thought." As she passed Joseph she smiled and shook her head. "You are absolutely crazy."

"I'm here to serve." Joseph laughed and folded up the stool. "This stuff goes on the back porch. I'll follow you."

After everything was in its proper place, they began to set the table. "Put out four places," Aunt Sylvi directed. "Vincent will be here soon."

"Vincent is here!" Gordy popped into the dining room.

"Whoa!" Joseph yelled and dropped a spoon on the table. "You scared me."

"Sorry, little man." He hugged Joseph around the shoulder with one arm and messed up his hair with the other. "And who is your friend?"

"Hi, I'm Constance," she said with an uncertain smile.

He reached out to shake her hand. "Pleased to make your acquaintance, Constance." He pulled out a chair at the end of the table and took a seat. "Are you new to the neighborhood?"

"Goodness no, Vincent." Aunt Sylvi burst through the door with a large bowl of steaming pasta. "You know Zita from my card club? Constance is her granddaughter." As she turned back to the kitchen, she gave Connie a wink. "She's going to be staying a few days while her parents are out of town."

Joseph and Connie exchanged a grin. Good old Aunt Sylvi.

"Have a seat and get ready for the best meatballs you've ever eaten," Gordy said to the kids. "How have you been, little man?" Aunt Sylvi and the kids had a seat and passed the food. "How are your studies?" Vincent continued.

"Good, Uncle Gordy. Science and grammar are my best subjects."

"Grammar? You're smarter than me, kid." Gordy reached for the meatballs, and Aunt Sylvi noticed a bandage on his hand. "Gracious, son, what have you done to yourself?"

He seemed startled for a moment and quickly pulled his hand back. "Oh, I burned it on an engine at the shop." He looked down. Connie picked up the meatballs and passed them to him. He smiled at her and nodded.

"Be more careful, son. Please, pass the sauce to Connie. Oh, and we have a special occasion tonight! We are celebrating her birthday. I've made a gorgeous cake for dessert." Aunt Sylvi giggled and looked at Joseph. "And you know"—she looked at Connie—"I found even more flour on the floor of my bedroom! I don't think I'll ever get it all cleaned up."

The conversation during the meal was light-hearted. They discussed Joseph's studies and his activities since his last visit. Connie enjoyed observing; it was almost as if she wasn't there. She just listened to the conversation. She observed how they talked and what they talked about while looking around the room at Aunt Sylvi's things.

She liked the way the table looked. Once again, she had enjoyed picking out the tablecloth. This time Aunt Sylvi chose plain white dishes. So, Connie decided on the lavender tablecloth with small white and yellow flowers. Joseph said it was "girly," which made Connie want to use it all the more.

When Aunt Sylvi saw the tablecloth she chose, she got out some beautiful yellow glasses. They were clear on the bottom and gradually tapered into yellow toward the top.

Joseph jokingly complained that there had never been any fancy glasses brought out for his visits before. Aunt Sylvi said she didn't realize he cared about fancy glasses. She told Joseph that it made her feel like she and Connie were having a tea party. He just rolled his eyes at her. Connie smiled as she thought about it. Then she noticed Joseph had already spilled sauce on the beautiful table setting. Figures. There goes the tea party.

Finally, Uncle Gordy folded his napkin and placed it on his plate. "Ma, thank you! It was as wonderful as ever. I'm glad you're here Joey and Connie. It was a pleasure. But if you will excuse me, I need to be going."

"Oh, Vincent. You have been going and going so much lately. Can't you stay and have birthday cake?" Aunt Sylvi pleaded.

"Sorry, Ma." He kissed her cheek. "I've got a date." He raised his eyebrows to Joseph and Joseph smiled.

Aunt Sylvi rose and followed him into the kitchen. Connie and Joseph could hear them. "You are going to see that Nancy Gibson again, aren't you? Vincent, you know how I feel about that girl. The cigarettes and all the makeup. She is nowhere near a lady."

"Ma, Nancy Gibson is a nice girl." He returned to the dining room to finish his glass of water. He set the glass down, smiled, and gave Joseph a wink. "She goes to church, Ma! What more do you want?"

Aunt Sylvi entered the room with the birthday cake. "Going to church doesn't make you a nice girl any more than sitting in a tree makes you a bird." This made Connie chuckle. But not for long when she realized how serious Aunt Sylvi was. "It takes more than just going to church, although it wouldn't hurt you to attend mass every now and then. Father Thomas asks about you every Sunday."

"Ah, come on, Ma!" Vincent nuzzled her neck, teasing her.

"Enough!" Aunt Sylvi lifted her hands. "That is enough!"

Gordy smiled and looked back at Joseph one more time. "Why don't you kids ride on over to the station tomorrow. Bring some sandwiches and we can walk over to the park for lunch. We'll watch them set up for the carnival."

"Gee, that sounds swell, Uncle Gordy. We might just do that."

"All right. Who wants ice cream?" Aunt Sylvi asked on her way into the kitchen. "Bring those dirty plates in, dears, and we will have our birthday treat now!"

"And we can play Monopoly after cake!" Joseph grabbed an empty serving bowl.

"No! No Monopoly!" Connie protested. "How about some cards, Joseph? Aunt Sylvi said there is a deck in the hall table drawer."

Joseph agreed to cards, but they couldn't agree on a game. Aunt Sylvi was determined to teach them Gin Rummy. However, after nearly twenty minutes, she had everyone so confused she decided they would be better off playing either Slapjack or War. They decided on Slapjack.

Hours of Slapjack, in fact, and the most delicious chocolate cake Connie had ever eaten. She must have thanked Aunt Sylvi eight or nine times. The cake with the fluffy frosting back home didn't even come to mind as she ate this one. Actually, all thoughts of home were miles away.

As the Slapjack game continued, Connie was surprised how intensely Joseph played. They didn't even see Aunt Sylvi leave to take her bath. "Shh! Listen!" Joseph said to Connie.

"What is it?" She froze in her chair, startled.

"Bath water. Aunt Sylvi is running a bath."

"You scared me. Don't do that again. So what if Aunt Sylvi is running a bath? She's a clean woman. You should try it sometime." Connie smiled.

"Oh no, young innocent one. It means no one is guarding the cake!"

"Aha! I'm with you now, brother! Feeling like a second piece now, are you?"

"Don't mind if I do, madame. Thank you for asking."

Joseph opened the cabinet where Aunt Sylvi had gotten the small plates and handed one to Connie. "Your Highness," he said loftily. She curtsied as she took it from him. He took one for himself and sliced into the cake. "How much do you want?"

"Medium-small," Connie replied as she held out her plate.

"Hm. That looks about medium-small to me." He plopped a piece on her plate and returned for a piece of his own.

"Holy cow! This is definitely more like medium-large!" Connie protested.

"Just sit down and eat it!" He laughed and cut himself a piece, then took his plate to the table where they both ate most of the frosting first.

Connie pushed her plate away. "Blah! I can't eat all of this! I think I'm going to throw up!" She laughed and held her stomach.

"Come on, Connie! You can do it! Look at me! Eating my frosting like a man!" They both laughed. "I bet I can finish mine before you can finish yours."

"No way," Connie challenged. "Both of your pieces were three times the size of mine. Plus, I'm telling you, I'm going to vomit if I eat one more bite."

"What a baby! What a little chocolate cake baby!" Joseph teased.

"Where are you sleeping tonight?" she asked.

"Your floor. Why?"

"Okay then. If I get sick, it's coming your way. On your mark, get set, go!" she yelled and stuffed cake into her mouth.

"Hey! Wait!" Joseph laughed and put his face in his plate.

After a few seconds, Connie threw her hands in the air and yelled, "The winner!"

"You have to swallow!" Joseph cried, "I can still win!" He shoved the last part of his cake in his mouth, then stopped and looked at Connie. She was laughing so hard her body was shaking, but no sound was coming out of her mouth.

"Are you okay?" he asked, his mouth completely full.

Still laughing she shook her head. Through the cake she did her best to say, "I can't swallow! Need milk!"

That made Joseph begin to laugh. "Spit it out!" He managed to say with his cheeks bulging.

"Can't. It's stuck," she said. "You look like a chipmunk." They both laughed harder. Joseph got up to get the milk. By this time there were tears streaming down their cheeks. He poured them each a glass and set the milk bottle on the table.

Still laughing, they tried drinking, chewing, and swallowing until all the cake was gone. Connie had frosting in her hair and cake all over her mouth. Joseph had frosting on his nose and cake mixed with milk dripping from the bandage on his chin. There were cake crumbs all over the table and floor, as well as on their hands and clothes. They were having so much fun they didn't notice that Aunt Sylvi had entered the kitchen. Suddenly, the smell of lavender lotion announced her presence, and the laughter stopped immediately. Slowly, they turned to face her.

She looked at their chocolate-covered faces. She had been prepared to scold them, but at the moment she was trying her best not to laugh. Finally, she said, "I am looking at you two and this mess in my kitchen, which I had already cleaned, and I only have one question for you." She paused for a moment. They hung their heads and waited. "My question is . . . who won?"

Aunt Sylvi shook her head and smiled. Connie and Joseph were stunned. Finally, they both smiled with relief. "I think I will just have a seat over here," Aunt Sylvi continued, "while you two get this mess cleaned up."

"Yes, ma'am," they said and went to work. As they cleaned, they told Aunt Sylvi all about what happened. Connie had never had so much fun cleaning.

Once the kitchen was spotless, they took their baths and crawled into their beds. Aunt Sylvi sat on Connie's bed to say goodnight to them both. "Are you sure you wouldn't be more comfortable in your own bed, son?" she asked Joseph.

"No, thanks. I'll keep Connie company, Aunt Sylvi."

"And that's all right with you, dear?"

"Believe it or not, I do feel better when Joseph is here." Connie smiled at Aunt Sylvi.

"Well, all right then, little ones. I pray the Lord keeps you safe and gives you rest." She leaned over and gave Connie a kiss on the forehead. "Don't expect me to come down there, boy!" They laughed as Joseph stood up to give Aunt Sylvi a kiss and a hug.

"I love you," he said during their squeeze.

"Oh, I love you, my dearest." She held him out in front of her and squeezed his face with her hand. "Now, off to bed you chocolate monsters."

They all laughed as Aunt Sylvi turned out the light.

"Hey," Connie said, peeking over the edge of the bed. "Mind if I pray?"

"Go ahead." Joseph nodded, assuming she would pray silently as she had before on the steps. He was surprised when she asked for his hand.

"Dear Lord," Connie began, "thank You for keeping us safe today. Please protect us tonight as we sleep. Lord, please give Detective Rafferty wisdom, help me to get home, and Lord, please do something about Joseph's bad breath."

"Hey!" He pulled his hand away.

"Shush! I'm praying." Connie smiled and added, "Amen."

"You shouldn't do that!" Joseph rolled over to face the other way.

"Do what?"

"Joke with God! It's not funny!"

"I disagree," she said, still smiling. "I believe God has a terrific sense of humor. I think He thinks I am hilarious." There was silence for a moment. "Joseph?" Still silence. "I'm sorry. I was just playing around. I didn't mean to make you mad. You're the best boy friend I ever had."

"I am not your boyfriend!" Joseph snapped.

"Oh, take it easy! I meant friend who is a boy! Keep being ugly and I might just change my mind!"

"Jeepers," he said quietly.

"Hey!" Connie shouted suddenly as if she just had a brilliant idea.

"What is it?" Joseph snapped, rolling over to face her. "Are you ever going to sleep?"

"Do you think you will ever get married?" she asked in a dreamy voice.

"Sure. What a question! Where do you come up with these? Are all girls like this?" He settled back into his covers. "I'm going to marry Katherine Rose O'Malley."

"What? You're only twelve!"

"Well, I'm not going to marry her tomorrow. But I am certain she is the one I will marry."

"How do you know?" Constance was back in the dreamy voice again.

"I don't know. I just do."

"I wish I could be at your wedding," she mumbled sleepily.

"Me, too, Connie. I will miss you."

Morning came sooner than Joseph and Connie expected. They both lay there with thoughts of their plan for the day. Joseph imagined that he would sneak through the hall without Aunt Sylvi noticing. He would duck through doorways and peer around corners. Connie imagined quietly going through Uncle Gordy's dresser like she had seen on television.

Finally, they realized the other was awake and began to discuss how they could successfully complete their mission.

"What exactly are we looking for?" Joseph asked.

"I don't know. Anything that tells us where your uncle was the night of the break-in. Maybe something with the date on it. Like a ticket or a receipt. Anything to prove he wasn't in Aunt Sylvi's room that night."

Joseph nodded. "Okay. Let's go eat." He crawled out of his sleeping bag and made his way to the door.

"I swear you have a one-track mind!" She threw back her sheets. "I'll be right there. I want to put on my day clothes first."

"Good idea! Me too!" He closed the door behind him.

"Dork!" She laughed.

Connie waited at the top of the stairs for what seemed to be an hour. Finally, Joseph appeared in the hallway. "Have trouble picking out an outfit?" she asked.

"Gee! Are all girls from the future this sassy?" He smirked as he walked past her down the stairs. "I heard the 'dork' comment by the way."

As they approached the doorway, Connie and Joseph could hear Aunt Sylvi and Gordy. They looked at each other cautiously, afraid they would act weird around Gordy and somehow give away the plan. But their mood changed as they spied Aunt Sylvi's blueberry muffins.

"Good morning, you two," Aunt Sylvi said with a smile. "And how did you both sleep last night?"

"Not bad at all," Joseph answered as he sat down at the kitchen table.

"I slept great, Aunt Sylvi. Thank you!" Connie tried not to make eye contact with Gordy.

"What's on the schedule for today?" Gordy asked.

"Uh, we're . . . uh . . ." Joseph froze for a moment and looked at Connie. She looked back at him with wide eyes as if to give him a mental nudge. "We're going to head out on the bikes. Probably meet up with Pete and Sonny. Maybe play a little stick," he finished casually.

"Don't forget the carnival is setting up today. Come by the station and I'll walk over with you," Uncle Gordy reminded them.

"Sure. That would be great." Joseph tried to sound excited. "I'm just not sure what the fellas will want to do."

"Who wants eggs and sausage?" Aunt Sylvi interrupted.

"I do!" Joseph and Connie cried.

"Gee, you kids sure are wound up today," Gordy chuckled. "Thanks for the grub, Ma! I need to make a call. Okay if I use the phone for a few minutes?"

"Certainly, dear. I've already made my morning calls to the ladies. We are meeting at the community center later for cards."

Gordy got up from the table and went to use the phone by the back door. Joseph began to talk, but Connie paid no attention. She wanted to concentrate on Gordy's conversation. "Yeah, it's me," she heard him say. "I'm working on it. I need more time. I should hear back from Smithers tomorrow."

"Hey! Connie!" Joseph raised his voice. She tried to hear the rest of Gordy's conversation, but he hung up.

"Hey! Wake up!" Joseph continued.

"I *am* awake!" she said with a glare. "I was concentrating."

"Are you almost done?" he inquired.

"I am. Thanks, Aunt Sylvi." Connie took her plate to the sink. "Do you need help with the dishes?"

"I'm fine, thank you. You two run along."

"Thanks, Aunt Sylvi. Would it be okay if we took the rest of the muffins upstairs?" Joseph asked.

"Of course, dear. But before you go up, come here and let me see your chin this morning." Sylvi lifted his face and took a good look at the cut. "I just want to make sure you got it nice and clean after last night. Now, you can leave the bandage off, but leave Uncle Sal's tape on there."

"I know, Aunt Sylvi. 'Don't take off Uncle Sal's tape until the cut has healed completely.'"

"Don't be a smarty pants!" she said as she squeezed his chin a little. "Now go on." She turned his head, kissed his cheek, and let him go.

"Thanks," Joseph said as he ran off.

They stopped at the top of the stairs and waited for Uncle Gordy to leave. "I think we should tell Pete and Sonny about you today," Joseph whispered.

"Really?" Connie was surprised.

"Shush!" Joseph put a finger to his lips. "Here he comes!"

They could hear footsteps. Suddenly Gordy appeared from the hallway. "Bye, Ma! See you later." And he walked out the front door.

"Goodbye, dear!" Aunt Sylvi called from the kitchen.

"Okay, now's our chance. Let's go!" Joseph directed.

"Wait! I need to do something with these muffins!" Connie was flustered.

"Just put them down!"

"What if Aunt Sylvi finds them. She will know we aren't in the attic!"

"Then hide them," he suggested.

"Where?" She turned left, then right, up one stair, then down again.

"For heaven's sake! Give them to me. I'll just eat them," Joseph grumbled.

"There's, like, seven of them!" She couldn't believe the plan was going to be ruined over muffins!

"Okay. Put them in my room!"

"Got it. Good idea." She ran down the hall and back again when suddenly a loud clap of thunder boomed!

"Ahh!" Connie squealed.

They both covered their ears and crouched down in the hallway.

"Okay, deep breath," Connie said. "It's just a storm. Let's go."

"All right. Follow me. Stay close. And keep watch for Aunt Sylvi." Once again Joseph gave the directions. He began his way down the stairs. He walked sideways with his back against the railing. Connie followed closely behind; her eyes shifted from side to side. They could hear the rain outside. She realized the sound of the rain was almost as loud as the whistling noise that Joseph was making with his nose every time he breathed.

"Your nose is whistling," Connie whispered as they stopped against the wall to peek into the kitchen.

"I have allergies," Joseph replied.

"Can't you breathe through your mouth or something? You're making me nervous!"

"I'll try." He spied Aunt Sylvi with her back to them as she washed dishes at the sink. "Coast is clear. Let's go." Quickly and quietly, they tiptoed past the kitchen, down the hall, and into Uncle Gordy's bedroom.

"Oh my goodness. This is crazy!" Connie panted. "I can hardly catch my breath."

"Let's hurry. You start here. I'll start over there." Joseph pointed to the opposite side of the room. *Boom!* Another clap of thunder gave them both a jolt.

"Jeepers! I should have gone to the bathroom before we came in here!" Connie joked nervously.

"Funny! Just start looking!" Joseph wasn't in the mood for jokes.

Suddenly, they heard the front door open. They both froze and stared at each other. Heavy footsteps sounded down the hall. Connie's eyes grew wide.

"It's just me, Ma. I forgot my wallet. It's really starting to come down out there!" Gordy's voice carried over the sound of the pouring rain.

Silently, Connie made a horrible face and began to dance around. Joseph motioned toward the bed. She nodded. They dove under as quickly as they could, just as Uncle Gordy entered his bedroom. From under the bed, they could see his feet. They watched him walk to the front of his dresser.

"Gordano, Gordano, Gordano," he said, talking to himself. "How did you get yourself in such a mess?" They looked at each other and listened.

Heee hahh heee hahh. Joseph's nose whistled until Connie reached over and pinched it shut.

"Just a few more days and this will all be over," Gordy said as he put his wallet in his pocket. He left his bedroom and closed the door behind him.

Joseph pushed Connie's arm away. "Are you trying to kill me?" he gasped.

"Can you *not* breathe through your mouth? Your whistling almost gave us away!"

"I think we should stay here until we hear him leave the house, and until I catch my breath! You pinched me hard!" Joseph whined as he rubbed his nose.

They stayed under the bed for a few more seconds to listen for the front door when Connie made a discovery.

"Joseph! Look! Our first clue!" Right beside her head was an old pair of blue canvas tennis shoes. "Take a look at these."

"So? They're just Uncle Gordy's sneakers. You call that a clue?"

"Look down here." Near the bottom and on the soles was a fine white dust. Flour! They crawled out from under the bed, and Constance carefully brought the shoes with her.

"I don't understand. Aunt Sylvi spilled the flour." Joseph was confused.

"Aunt Sylvi spilled flour in the kitchen, and we cleaned it up. She went to change her clothes and got cleaned up in her bedroom. She said there was so much flour on her it made a huge mess in her room and she didn't get it all cleaned up that night," Connie explained impatiently. "That was the night that her jewels were stolen. I know you don't want to hear it, but Gordy just said he had gotten himself into a mess. And these shoes prove he was in Aunt Sylvi's room the night of the robbery."

"I don't know, Connie. It just doesn't sound like Uncle Gordy. Let's take the shoes up to the attic and put them in the evidence bags. I just want to get out of here."

Joseph gradually opened the door with Connie pressed against his back. He leaned out and peered down the hall when the thunder crashed again. *Boom!* Both Joseph and Connie jumped and ran down the hall, up the stairs, and straight to the attic.

Out of breath, they sat side by side on the sofa. *Heee hahh. Heee hahh.* Joseph's nose wheezed again.

"Come on! Breathe through your mouth, please!" Connie was fed up!

Heee hahh. Heee hahh. "I can't help it. Did you get the shoes?"

"Yes, right here." She held them up carefully with her pinkies in the air.

Heee. "How about the muffins?" *Hahh.*

"No, still in your room." Connie sat the shoes down beside the sofa.

"Dratz. You'll have to get those later."

"Me? I'm not going anywhere, Whistles." *Creeeak!* They heard the attic door open slowly.

"What was that?" Connie scooted closer to Joseph.

"I don't know," Joseph answered with eyes as big as saucers. They heard footsteps. Someone was coming into the attic. Slowly. What should they do? Should they hide? There was no time. Joseph pulled Connie onto the floor. Maybe they would have time to run down the steps and out the door.

"Get ready to run," he mouthed to her. She nodded. The room was darker than normal because of the storm outside. Was it Uncle Gordy? No! It sounded like two sets of footsteps. Connie could hear her heart beating over Joseph's nose whistle. The footsteps were closer now. They were near the sofa. Closer. Closer. And then . . .

"Ahh!" Pete and Sonny jumped over the back of the sofa, and Joseph and Connie scrambled in fright.

Pete and Sonny fell to the floor in fits of laughter. They never dreamed they would give Joseph and Connie such a good scare. Joseph and Connie on the other hand, were not amused. Constance tried not to cry as she put Uncle Gordy's shoes in an evidence bag. Joseph sat down and thought that he just might throw up.

CHAPTER 7

Dreams

Finally, after Joseph calmed down from the fright Pete and Sonny had given him and Connie, he explained how they had just sneaked into Uncle Gordy's room.

"Wow! No wonder you were so scared. I feel kind of bad now." Sonny looked at Connie. "I'm really sorry, Connie. Are you okay?"

"Thanks." She smiled. "I'm okay now. Just kind of creeped out."

"Speaking of creeped out," Pete interrupted, "does anyone else hear that whistling sound?"

Connie burst into laughter. "It's Joseph's nose!"

"You are kidding me! Gordano, is that really your nose? You could join the circus with that or something! Teach me to do it!"

"Come on! It's allergies! I can't help it." Joseph changed the subject. "Hey, we have muffins in my bedroom. I'll be right back!"

While Joseph was gone, the three friends settled down and continued to discuss the possibilities of Uncle Gordy's involvement in the break-in.

"It seems so unlike him to be involved in something like this," Sonny explained to Connie as Joseph entered the room with the plate of blueberry muffins.

"Smile, Muffin Man!" Pete took his picture. "I still can't believe you two were under his bed when he came in the room!" he exclaimed as he leaned up to grab a muffin from the passing plate.

"It was crazy." Connie shook her head and made room for Joseph on the sofa.

"Hey, wait a minute! Aren't those my shirts you two are wearing?" Joseph inquired.

"We got stuck in the rain. Aunt Sylvi gave us a couple of yours to borrow. She was folding the laundry," Sonny explained.

Pete stood and struck a pose. "Bet you never imagined your clothes could ever look so good!" He held out his camera and took a picture of himself. Everyone laughed. "Gee, finally a summer with some excitement around here!" He plopped back down in the chair. "Okay, now a group shot!"

"Pete! You're killing me!" Joseph playfully fell backward on the sofa.

"You'll want to remember these moments! I'm telling you. You will be glad we did."

After Pete took his picture, Joseph stood and looked at Connie. "Actually, we have something else exciting to tell you," Joseph began. She scooted toward him. "It's about Connie and how she got here." Pete took a quick picture of her. "Pete!"

"What do you mean, 'how she got here'?" Sonny asked.

"You take the bus or something?" Pete looked up from his developing picture.

"Did someone drop you off?" Sonny guessed.

"No, um . . . Connie actually came through the closet." Joseph waited for a response.

"Huh?" Pete cocked his head.

"What?" Sonny scrunched his face.

"Well . . ." Joseph began, looking at Connie in desperation. This might be harder than he thought.

"Okay, let me add in more details." Connie popped off the sofa and began to pace. "It all started when I was playing in the closet at my grandpa's house."

"Where does he live?" Pete asked.

"He's dead," Joseph blurted.

Connie stopped pacing and glared at him, and Pete stared at her with his mouth open.

"When did he die?" Sonny asked with concern.

"In 2006," she said timidly as she waited for their reaction.

"What?" they both exclaimed.

"See, that's the thing," Joseph interjected.

"Let me get this straight." Sonny was trying hard. "You came here through a closet in your grandpa's house, who died fifty years in the future?"

"Forty-seven years to be exact," Connie corrected.

"Okay, who died in forty-seven years," Sonny repeated sarcastically.

"Exactly!" Connie smiled and clapped her hands. Her smile quickly faded as she realized it would not be quite that easy to convince them.

Pete's mouth still hung open.

Joseph looked at Connie. "Go get your backpack, Connie. We need the magazine."

"Got it." Her backpack was over by the window. The three boys watched as she made her way back to the sofa and unzipped her pack.

With his eyebrows raised, Sonny stretched his neck as far as he could. *What could possibly be in there? Is this some kind of joke?*

Connie handed the magazine to Joseph. "Magazine," she said as if she were a nurse assisting in a surgery.

"We don't know how it happened"—Joseph looked at Connie—"and we have not figured out how to get her back, but this is an honest-to-goodness magazine that Connie had with her when she fell through her grandpa's closet and landed in Aunt Sylvi's. Look right here at the year. It says May 2006."

Both boys were silent. Finally, Sonny said, "I don't know what to say. I'm kind of breathing funny."

Connie giggled. "Aunt Sylvi fainted."

"Connie, does that mean I am forty-seven years older than you?" Sonny asked softly.

She nodded. They stared at each other for a moment. A moment that was interrupted by Joseph.

"Disgusting, isn't it? To think you two could have been sweet on each other!"

"Joseph!" Connie was appalled that he would say such a thing.

"It's okay." Sonny grabbed her hand. "I can be sweet on you while I'm twelve, can't I?"

"I guess." She giggled again.

"I am sick!" Joseph made dramatic gagging sounds.

"Speaking of sick"—Sonny changed the topic quickly—"do you think Pete is all right?" The three friends looked at him. He'd had the same blank stare on his face for several minutes.

"Petie! Are you okay?" Joseph waved a hand before Pete's eyes.

"Is he breathing?" Connie looked over Joseph's shoulder.

"I think so. His stomach is moving. At least he stopped taking pictures," Joseph added.

"Joseph!" Connie snapped.

"Maybe you should punch him," Sonny suggested.

"I'm not going to punch him! He will knock me out! You punch him!" Joseph replied sharply.

"Nobody punch him! Just give him a little shake." Connie moved toward Pete. "Like this." She gently shook him by the shoulder. "Pete, sweetie. Are you okay? Pete!" She shook him a little harder until Joseph finally shoved him back into the chair.

"Pete!" Joseph yelled.

"Yeah! Right!" Pete stuttered. The three friends laughed, relieved.

"Hey Petie! Are you with us?" Sonny bent down and looked in his face. "It's all true! You have to hear this!"

The four friends sat and talked until lunchtime. Aunt Sylvi had gone to play cards at the center but left salami and fresh bread for sandwiches. The sky was still dark, and the rain fell steadily into the afternoon. To Connie's dismay, the boys decided to play a game of Monopoly. She reluctantly agreed and was alarmed to discover that Sonny and Pete played as competitively as Joseph. Pete bought several hotels, and Joseph owned Boardwalk and Park Place, but it was Sonny who managed to win the game.

Exhausted from the excitement, they all began to relax. Outside, the rain continued to fall while the dark clouds seemed to hang over Aunt Sylvi's house. One by one, the friends began to drift off to sleep.

"Gordano! Gordano!" Joseph heard in a dream. Was someone calling him? Who was it? Pete? Sonny? "Gordano! Vincent Gordano!" Someone was looking for Uncle Gordy. Oh no! It was the Barcolli Brothers. "Run, Uncle Gordy, run!" Joseph was in the alley behind Aunt Sylvi's house. He was running as fast as he could, but he wasn't moving at all. Who was he chasing? Or was someone chasing him?

Slowly, a police car pulled up beside him. It was Detective Rafferty in a patrolman's uniform. He was eating snickerdoodles. "We are looking for Vincent Gordano. We need to apologize to him. There was a big mistake. It wasn't your Uncle Gordy after all. He's innocent. He's innocent . . ."

"Constance, dear. You will be late for your senior prom," her mother called to her as she wandered into the kitchen of her grandpa's house. She admired her reflection in the oven door. She had waited all these years to be seventeen, and now she finally was. Her pink sequin dress was gorgeous. She was gorgeous. She liked her seventeen-year-old body! Wow!

"Come on, hon." It was Sonny. "Our dinner reservations are for six thirty. We don't want to keep everyone waiting."

"Let me just get your flower, Sonny!" Connie answered as she closed the refrigerator door and practically floated into the living room. "Here I am!" She pinned the flower on the tuxedo of the old white-haired man.

"I am so sorry, Connie," Sonny said in his dream. "Really, I am. I'm sorry you are stuck here forever and cannot get back home. But now you can be my sweetheart forever, and you can live in Aunt Sylvi's attic! Forever and ever and ever . . ."

"I'll have a strawberry malted, a double cheese-burger, and an order of onion rings," Pete told the lady with yellow hair. *"And a hot fudge sundae."*

Clang! Bang! A noise from downstairs gave Sonny, Joseph, and Connie a jolt.

"Did you hear something?" Joseph jumped up.

"I don't know." Connie stretched. "I fell asleep."

"Me too," Sonny said.

"I think we all fell asleep." Joseph needed a big stretch too.

"I had the strangest dream," everyone said at once.

"Me too!" they all replied with a laugh.

"With a cherry on top, please." Pete smiled, still deep in his dream. They looked at him and laughed even harder.

Clang! Bang! "There it is again." Joseph looked concerned. Connie ran to the windows. There were no cars outside.

"Maybe Aunt Sylvi is home," Sonny suggested. "Connie, you stay up here with Sleeping Beauty. Joseph, let's go down and check it out."

"Sure," Joseph agreed and looked back at Connie.

"Be careful," she told them.

Slowly, the boys crept down the attic steps into the hallway and down the staircase. *Clang! Bang!* They both stopped for a moment until they finally heard Aunt Sylvi. "Get out of there you nasty old thing, before I give you a good wallop!"

"Aunt Sylvi! Are you all right?" Joseph ran to her. She was on the kitchen floor, halfway in the cabinet.

"Oh my!" She giggled and peered out at the boys. "Hello, Sonny. What are you dears up to?"

"Well, Aunt Sylvi"—Sonny knelt beside her—"Maybe we should ask you that question."

"Me?" She continued to giggle. "I'm having myself a fight with my large mixer, and I'm afraid it is about to win."

"Why don't you let us get that out for you, Aunt Sylvi?" Joseph suggested.

"Thank you, boys," she said as they helped her up. "The rain has stopped and the sun is finally out. Joseph, why don't you kids run down to the carnival?" She reached into her apron pocket. "Here is some spending money for you all. It should be enough for dinner and some treats as well. Just put that over in the corner," she directed as Joseph lugged the big metal mixer to the counter. "Thank you, dears. Now you all hurry along and enjoy the carnival."

"Thanks, Aunt Sylvi!" Joseph kissed her on the cheek and ran from the kitchen.

"Yes, thanks." Sonny did the same.

"Goodness, me!" Sylvi exclaimed and put her hand to her cheek. "Now, mister," she said to the mixer, "it's just you and me!"

"Guys! Guys!" Joseph yelled as he made his way up to the attic. "The sun is out! Let's go to the carnival!"

Connie stood at the top of the steps. "I am guessing that everything is safe downstairs?"

"Oh, that? Yes. That was just Aunt Sylvi. Have you looked outside?" He ran to the windows. "Let's go! Let's go! This year I want to play every game on the Midway!"

"This year we have someone to win stuffed animals for!" Sonny smiled at Connie. She smiled back.

"Stuffed animals?" Joseph looked at Sonny, then Connie, then back at Sonny. "I guess that would be all right." He studied them closely and glanced down at Pete. "Are you kidding me? Is Pete still dreaming of ice cream sundaes?"

"I think he moved on to baked goods while you two were downstairs." Connie laughed.

"Pete!" Sonny yelled. "Let's go!"

"I am right behind you!" Pete cried and jumped from his chair.

Joseph laughed while Connie looked at Sonny in amazement. "Why didn't that work the last time?"

"Where are we going?" Pete asked as if he had been awake for hours.

"Carnival!" Joseph answered with excitement. "Let's grab a Popsicle on the way out." He led the group from the attic. Pete and Sonny were close behind, and Connie scurried to keep up.

"Orange! Orange!" the boys chanted.

"Nice try!" Joseph shouted. "The orange ones are mine. You know I have eternal dibs!"

"This is crazy!" Connie muttered. On the back porch, Sonny and Pete stopped to pick up their bikes. Joseph and Connie went out to the garage. When Joseph opened the door, she was again baffled by more of the mysterious white chalk-like substance on the floor. "I am going to figure out what this is! You just watch! I will figure this out!"

"You do that, Sherlock!" Joseph walked his bike past her and out the door. "I am going to the carnival."

"I'm coming! I'm going!" She grabbed her bike and quickly followed behind.

The boys rode on ahead. They laughed and stood as they pedaled. Finally, they all sat down and began to coast. As if on cue, the three raised their hands in the air and rode without steering.

Someone shouted, "Midway, here we come!"

Connie knew she was in for the adventure of a lifetime!

CHAPTER 8

The Carnival

Connie could feel the excitement in the air as they pedaled closer and closer to the carnival. They turned one last corner, and she could see the rides up ahead. She began to hear music and game keepers calling out, "Step right up and try your luck!" "Teeco tickets just twenty-five cents!"

"What's a Teeco ticket?" Connie asked Joseph as they began to slow their bikes down.

"They get you into the carnival. Let's ditch our bikes over here in the grass." Joseph led the way, and the boys jumped off their bikes as if their seats were on fire.

"It's really muddy over here!" Connie observed as she slowly dismounted.

"It's been pouring all day." Joseph smirked, looking around. "It's really muddy everywhere."

"You guys just dropped your bikes in the mud. Maybe you should have used your kickstands or something," she suggested.

"Go ahead," Joseph mocked, "use your kickstand."

116

She carefully parked her bike, set the kickstand, and walked away. Slowly the kickstand began to sink until the bike toppled over.

"And there you go. That's why we don't use our kickstands in the mud," Joseph remarked.

She passed in front of him and smiled. "Thank you. Lesson learned."

"What are we going to do first?" Pete asked. "I say we get something to eat."

"I don't care. I want to do everything!" Sonny lifted his arms in a sweeping motion.

"Food sounds great to me!" Joseph chimed in.

"I could eat!" Connie agreed, overwhelmed with excitement.

"I say we start with hot dogs and lemon ice! We can move on to the Teeco cakes and Chocolate Thunder later," Pete suggested.

"Mmm, Chocolate Thunder! I'll have two of those!" Connie giggled at Sonny.

Sonny leaned in close to her. "Last year, Gordano ate the Chocolate Thunder just before he rode the Octopus. He threw up during the entire ride! It was disgusting!"

"Oh, gross!" Connie groaned.

"Here we are!" Joseph announced.

The ticket booth was black with gold lettering across the top. It read, "Teeco's Tremendous." Beside the window in smaller writing it said, "Teeco Tickets 25 cents each." A quarter each? Connie could not believe it. Nothing costs a quarter in her time!

"I want a picture of you all by the ticket booth." Pete motioned for them to line up. They were used to the drill by now. "One, two, three! Great! Thanks! This is fantastic!" he said between clicks.

Inside the ticket booth was . . . someone. Connie guessed it to be Teeco. Teeco's hair was pulled up in a black sparkly turban with a gold jewel in the front. She was wearing heavy black makeup around her eyes and dark-red lipstick. At least the makeup made her *assume* Teeco was a woman. But everything else about the face made her think Teeco was a man. She (or he) was wearing a cape that matched the turban.

"May I please have four tickets?" Joseph asked as he placed his dollar bill through the window.

"Certainly," Teeco answered in an extremely low voice.

"Oh my goodness!" Connie giggled softly as they walked away from the booth. The boys seemed unaffected. Maybe they saw Teeco every year and were used to him. She shrugged. "So, where's the food?" she asked the boys.

"Right this way, my queen," Pete joked and jumped in front of her. He extended his elbow to escort her to the hotdog booth. "Uh, Connie," Pete lowered his voice.

"Yes, Pete?" Constance smiled.

"I don't . . . Well, I don't talk much to girls, really," Pete stammered. "But if I did, I mean, I wanted to talk to you and tell you that I think you are all right. And if you can't get back to your house through the closet, or however you got here . . . well, I'd be honored to be your friend."

"Pete, you are sweet." Connie hugged his arm. "Thank you. I think we are already friends. Is that okay?"

"Sure!" He blushed slightly then said, "Can you smell that? Can you? It's a Teeco dog! We're here!"

The boys each ordered foot-long hot dogs with chili and cheese. Connie remembered the story of Joseph and the Octopus and ordered a regular dog, minus the chili. With dogs and napkins in hand, they walked across the Midway to get a lemon ice.

"Hey, look!" Connie pointed to the sign beside the window that listed their choices. "They have Tang! When the astronauts go to the moon, they take Tang with them! Isn't that crazy?"

"What are you talking about?" Joseph looked at her as if she had lost her mind.

Sonny ordered lemon ices for everyone.

"Our astronauts make it to the moon, and they decide to take orange drink with them?" Joseph continued in disbelief.

"I know," Connie agreed. "I can think of a bunch of other things I would rather take as well." They laughed and sipped their lemon ice.

They stood while they ate, and while they ate, they laughed. Connie was impressed with their ability to hold their foot-long dogs in one hand and their drinks in the other. She did notice, however, that Pete was wearing part of his chili dog on the front of his shirt. Or was it Joseph's shirt? She couldn't remember.

Her focus left her friends and she began to look around at the people, the games, the rides—everything. The year 1959 was so different. She felt for a moment like she was forgetting what things were like at home. How long had she been gone? Aunt Jen must really be worried. Should she call Grandpa and leave a message? Would Aunt Jen even be born yet? Wait a minute . . . Call Grandpa? She had not thought of that possibility until now. Would Grandma still be alive? Maybe she could call and talk to both of them. But how would she explain who she was?

"Connie!" Joseph gave her a shake. "Are you ready to go to the Menagerie of Oddities?"

"Mwaaa Hahahaha!" The three boys all gave an evil laugh.

"What's with the Frankenstein laugh?" Connie asked.

"You have to do it every time someone says, 'Menagerie of Oddities,'" Joseph explained.

"Mwaaa Hahahaha!" they repeated.

"And its Dracula, by the way," Joseph corrected.

"Okay, so what is the . . ." She paused and looked at each of them. "The Menagerie of . . . you know," Connie said with a smile.

"Ah, come on!" Sonny joked.

"No fair," Pete protested.

"It's a tent full of glass jars containing strange and outrageous things." Joseph began to move his arms in a circular fashion as if to stir a large caldron. "A giant's eight-inch thumb!" Connie winced. "An unborn alligator with six eyes."

"What?" she said in disgust.

"Shrunken heads from the tribes of the unknown." Joseph waved his arms above his head.

"You are so dramatic. That all sounds absolutely disgusting. Why on earth would I want to go see something like that?" Connie demanded.

"Because the three of us are going and you are coming too!" Joseph grabbed her hand and they all ran to the Menagerie of Oddities tent.

The man at the ticket booth had a long black beard that hung way past his chest, but his head was completely bald. He wore a white poofy shirt that reminded Connie of a pirate. On top of his bald head sat a small brown cap. She didn't think he looked odd enough to be at the Menagerie. Until . . . he turned and she saw the large spider-web tattoo that covered the entire right side of his head. *And Mwaaa ha-ha to you too!* she thought. *Yikes!*

"Fifty cents each for the thrill of your life," the spider-web man said with absolutely no enthusiasm in his voice.

"Fifty cents!" Connie turned to Joseph. "This had better be good." Suddenly she began to appreciate the value of a quarter.

"You are going to love it!" Joseph told her. "Let's go!" Pete led the group, then the remaining three followed.

Inside were three rows of narrow tables, and on each table were glass jars of various sizes. Inside each glass jar was a different oddity, some of which floated in a clear, greenish liquid.

The entire place gave Connie the creeps. Who collected things like this? Everything looked ancient, including the jars and the tables. Plus, it smelled funny. She was glad to see that the boys didn't spend too much time at any one jar. The odor made her stomach sick. Joseph was right; there were three shrunken heads and an alligator fetus, but it only had four eyes. But there was no giant's thumb. However, they did have the world's longest fingernail, which curled around and around like a big corkscrew. They all agreed that it was completely disgusting. Other items in the Menagerie included:

A pig's eyeball
One-hundred-year-old ball of cow manure
A giant millipede
Siamese twin turtles connected at the shell
Shark's teeth
Two-headed iguana
A human lung
A human liver
A human kidney

As they exited the tent, Pete turned to Sonny. "I don't think it was as good as last year."

"Me neither," Sonny agreed.

"It was disgusting! That's what it was!" Connie was steamed. "I'd like to know whose body goes with those human organs in there! How absolutely disrespectful! I mean, you don't just keep human organs in a jar, set them next to Tippy and Tony the Siamese turtles, and charge people fifty cents to see them. That is just wrong!"

"Connie, I know just where I want to take you." Joseph looked at Pete and Sonny and laughed. He took her by the hand and led her down the Midway. The crowd was getting thicker and thicker, and the sun was seriously thinking about setting.

"Step right up and test your strength!" the man said. "Would you like to test your strength, son?" he asked Sonny.

"No, sir, but thank you. I believe our friend Connie would though." They pushed Connie forward.

"That will be twenty-five cents," the man said. Joseph handed him a quarter, and the man handed Connie what appeared to be a sledgehammer. "Do you think you can handle this, little lady? It's pretty heavy," he warned.

That just made her even madder. "Oh, I can handle it all right," Constance reassured him. She lifted the hammer high over her head and brought it down with all her might. The marker went about three quarters of the way to the top.

"Give the man another quarter!" Connie shouted. Once again, she lifted the hammer high over her head and brought it down with all her might. Again, it reached about three quarters of the way to the top. "One more!" she shouted.

"Jeepers! I can't believe Connie can still lift her arms," Sonny said to Joseph as he handed the man another quarter.

"Here she goes," Joseph encouraged. "This one is it."

Connie lifted it over her head. She swung it around and brought it down, but this time she made a low moaning sound. The hammer hit with a force not seen, and before she knew it, it went straight to the top. *Ding!* went the bell.

"Well, I'll be," said the man.

"I did it!" Connie screamed weakly with her hands in the air. Pete quickly took her picture.

"That was amazing!" Sonny shouted.

"Boy, were you mad!" Pete chuckled.

"You are something else, Connie!" Joseph put his arm around her and gave her a squeeze.

She smiled. "Thanks. I've always wondered if I could do that."

"Well, you can!" Pete said. "I know it's going to mess up the plans, but we just have to celebrate with a Chocolate Thunder!"

"Oh, hurray!" Connie clapped. "Let's do!" She truly could not believe she had done it. She was so proud of herself. She was also certain she would not be able to move her arms in the morning. But it was totally worth it.

They all ran and laughed their way to the Chocolate Thunder booth. Once they had ordered, they spied a small table that was unoccupied. "Hurry! Grab it!" Joseph cried as they all took off and ran. They were laughing so hard by the time they sat down that Connie had to wipe tears from her cheeks.

"I didn't think we were going to make it," she cackled. The sun had almost set completely, but the sky was lit by the many lights of the carnival. The boys teased her about her super-human strength. As they laughed, she jokingly asked, "Would someone please feed me my Chocolate, because I've totally lost my Thunder." That tickled *her* more than anyone, and she laughed so hard she almost lost her Thunder out her nose.

"Hello, boys and girls." They all looked up to see Uncle Gordy and a girl with big red hair approaching their table. Their jovial laughter became awkward and nervous. "Mind if we join you?" Everyone scooted around to make room for Gordy and his date. "Do you all know Nancy?"

Ah! The famous churchgoing, make-up-wearing, cigarette-smoking, Aunt-Sylvi-didn't-like-her Nancy, Connie thought. She had the giggles so bad and was trying hard not to laugh.

"Nancy, this is my nephew, Joey, his pals, Pete and Sonny, and his doll. What's your name again, sweetheart?"

"Constance," she said extending, her hand to Nancy. *Doll?* she thought. *How hilarious.*

"Charmed," Nancy said in a voice that sounded like a cartoon mouse. Pete acted startled, and they all looked at each other. No one dared to laugh.

Sonny wanted to hear her talk more. "So, Nancy," he said, "what is your favorite part of the carnival?"

"*Oooooo, heh heh heh heh heh heh,*" she said with a squeal. Her laugh was more like a crazy chipmunk than a mouse. "I especially like the ride that goes around and around."

"Oh, you mean the Ferris wheel?" Connie suggested helpfully.

"Sure, the Ferris wheel." Nancy agreed. "Heh heh heh heh heh. Now that's the one with the ponies, right?"

"No, no, that's the carousel, Nancy," Joseph explained. He felt like his sides were going to explode at any minute. He could hardly hold the laughter back.

Suddenly, Joseph and Connie noticed a look of fear on Gordy's face. They turned around just in time to see the Barcolli brothers disappear into the crowd. "Sorry, doll, but as fun as the conversation has been, it's time for us to go. See you kids later."

"Sure, Uncle Gordy. We'll see you later." Joseph and Connie looked at each other, then looked back out at the crowd.

"I'm kind of scared now. Should we leave?" Connie asked.

"I don't think so. They are after him, not us. We will be fine. Besides, we haven't ridden any rides yet!"

The other boys agreed with Joseph and reassured Connie that everything would be fine. Sonny even suggested that the Barcolli brothers were watching Gordy and probably left when he did.

They continued to sit at the same table after they had finished their Chocolate Thunders. It was a great location to plan the next few steps of their evening. They would ride the tilt-a-whirl as well as the bumper cars, but both were further down the Midway. They decided to play several games along the way too.

After the bumper cars would be the Ferris wheel. No one but Connie wanted to ride it. However, Sonny agreed to take her on it while Joseph and Pete went through the fun house.

That was as much as they had planned, but they all agreed it was a good plan. They took off for the Midway to discover the games that awaited them. As they ran off, none of them noticed the two familiar faces still lurking in the crowd.

Pete and Sonny first played games where coins were pushed off the top of a platform. Connie didn't understand that one. She and Joseph played one where they controlled a big claw and tried to maneuver it to pick up prizes. The first turn was Joseph's, and he was going for a shiny gold harmonica. He had it in the claw, but it dropped out at the very last second.

When it was Constance's turn, she told Joseph she was going for the little plastic baby doll. She didn't really see anything else that caught her eye.

"It's your turn," Joseph cheered her on. "Are you going for the doll? You can do it! Slow and easy."

Slow and easy was her plan, but she had changed her mind about the doll. She moved the claw closer and closer to the harmonica. Slowly, she picked it up and swung the arm around. She sat it down gently on the "out" tray and released it from the claw. Triumphantly, Connie reached for the harmonica and handed it to Joseph.

"Are you giving this to me?" he asked. Connie smiled and nodded.

"Fellas! Hey, fellas!" He ran over to Sonny and Pete, who had grown frustrated with their game. "Look what Connie won for me! Isn't it swell! A new harmonica!" Joseph attempted to play it a little.

Pete scowled. "Did she win you any lessons?"

"No!" Connie laughed. "I should have thought that through more clearly. Can we go over to the ring toss now?"

"Sure! Let's go!" Sonny jumped to the front of the group. "Come on!"

They followed Sonny through the crowded Midway and, single file, wove their way to the games. No less than three people behind Joseph were the Barcolli brothers. One by one they jumped out of the moving crowd. The Barcolli brothers, however, continued on for several feet, never letting the kids out of their sight.

The ring toss was five tries for ten cents. Joseph missed all tosses on his first try. "That's not possible. I want to go again." On his second round he got the first toss with no problem. However, the next four were not even close. "What?" he yelled as he put his hands on the top of his head.

"It's okay. It's just a silly game," Connie consoled.

"I should have done better." He was even more frustrated when the man told him he had won a genuine Teeco carnival bookmark. "How wonderful!" Joseph said sarcastically. "If I ever make it as a writer, I'll be sure to keep it in my first published book!"

Connie had never seen him this upset.

"I'll go next," Sonny said with his chest puffed out. Connie thought this was looking more and more like a competition.

"Now, guys. Let's just have fun. Okay?" she said to try and lighten the mood.

Sonny also missed every toss on his first try. "I think this game is rigged! I'm going again!" He placed another dime on the counter. He missed four out of five tosses. On the fifth toss the ring got hooked on the bottle and it looked good, but then it fell off at the last minute. "There is no way! There is just *no way*." Sonny slammed his fist on the countertop and turned to walk away.

"Your turn, Pete," Connie said cautiously.

"Are you nuts? I'm not even trying." Pete put his hands in the air to show he surrendered.

"I love this game! I'm giving it a try. You guys are just too competitive. I just think it is fun to try." Connie put her money on the counter. She lined up her first toss and let it go. *Clink!* Perfect shot around the bottle. She smiled, not sure if the boys were watching and afraid to turn around in case they were. She lined up her second shot. *Clink!* "Ohhhh!" She jumped up and clapped a little. The boys were watching now. *Clink!* Ring number three. "He-he!" Connie was getting excited.

"You can do it, Connie. Get them all!" Pete cheered as he snapped a quick photo. Sonny and Joseph were silent.

Clink! There went number four. "This is crazy!" she yelled. She felt a hand on her shoulder. It was Joseph.

"Show them what you're made of!" He gave her a squeeze.

Connie took a deep breath, lined up her throw, and tossed. *Clink!* "Oh my goodness! I did it! I can't believe it! I never win these things!"

The boys all gave her a hug, and the man behind the counter let her pick from the big stuffed animals on the top row.

"I'll pick the purple giraffe."

"Good choice, young lady. Congratulations!" The man got down her prize and handed it to her.

"Over here, Connie!" Pete needed to document the purple giraffe for sure!

"How about Connie and I head on over to the Ferris wheel, and you guys go on to the fun house? We'll meet you at the fried cake booth." Sonny was planning ahead. He did not want to leave without a fried cake!

"Woo-hoo! The fun house!" Pete threw his hands in the air.

"Let's go! We'll see you later!" Joseph smiled at Connie, just to make sure she was okay with it. She smiled back but blushed a little. She turned to Sonny, and they began to walk slowly to the Ferris wheel.

The split confused the Barcolli brothers. "Let's stick with the girl," the tall one said.

"Sure, the girl," the short one agreed, and they followed Sonny and Connie to the Ferris wheel.

"So, tell me what your life is like forty years from now!" Sonny wanted to learn more about Connie.

"Forty-seven years!" Connie teased. "It's really different." She felt kind of sad as she thought about it. "We can't ride our bikes around like you guys because it isn't safe anymore."

"What do you mean it isn't safe?" Sonny asked, confused.

"Our parents have to teach us about 'stranger danger' and to not trust anyone we don't know." She rolled her eyes.

"Why are people so scared?" Sonny didn't understand.

"I guess because there are a lot more mean people in the future than there are today. But there are still a lot of cool things that we have that you don't, like laptop computers and cable television. They have even figured out that chocolate is good for you! Well, dark chocolate, that is. It's crazy!" She laughed.

"Sounds great. I wish I could come visit." The Ferris wheel lights blinked green and white.

"You will be there one day. You'll just have to be patient." She smiled at him. "Hey, what happened at the eye doctor? Are you getting glasses or not?"

"Yeah, but they aren't so bad. The man said they will be ready in about a week."

"You'll look nice in glasses. I hope I get to see them." Connie smiled at him, then turned away.

"Thanks. I'm just excited about being able to see better at school."

"I'm sure that will be nice," she said without looking back. She had begun to feel slightly awkward.

They stopped in front of the Ferris wheel and stood side by side in line at the ticket booth. Their hands brushed softly. For a moment Connie thought Sonny just might hold her hand, when suddenly someone pushed their way between them. She gasped. It was one of the Barcolli brothers.

He was in her face. She could feel his breath on her neck. She backed up quickly but ran into something. Someone. It was the other brother, the bigger one. He grabbed her by the back of her hair. He pulled her head back so hard she was looking up at him. Tears streamed down her face. She had never been so scared. She didn't even realize she had dropped the purple giraffe.

"Hi, honey!" His voice was deep and scratchy. "Your friend Vinnie doesn't seem to be taking us seriously."

"Yeah, he's not too serious," the smaller brother repeated.

"So, we thought maybe you could explain to him the severity of this problem."

"Yeah, you 'splain things to him."

Sonny began to cry as he struggled to get to Connie, but they pushed him back.

"If we don't have our money tomorrow, his darling mother, Mrs. Gordano, might just have some problems of her own. Or who knows? Perhaps it will be you and your boyfriend Joseph with the problems."

"Yeah, you'll have problems of your own!" the short one repeated.

"Capeesh?" the big brother asked.

Connie nodded her head the best she could. He pulled her hair even tighter. "Okay," she managed to say. "Okay, I'll tell him. Please don't hurt us."

"Okay, doll." He lifted her by her hair all the way to her tiptoes. Connie let out a shriek. He winked at her, then let her go. Sonny screamed as she fell to the ground, and the Barcolli brothers disappeared into the crowd.

"Connie! Connie!" Sonny cried. "Are you okay?"

She reached for him to help her up. "We have to find Joseph and get home to Aunt Sylvi. We have to call Detective Rafferty. Hurry, Sonny! Hurry!"

They both ran as fast as they could, yet both were crying. Sonny was slightly ahead of Connie but he held her hand tightly. She trembled and her knees were weak. As they ran toward the fun house, she tripped and fell hard. Sonny stopped to help her up. "Your knees, Connie. They are really skinned up! You're bleeding."

"Don't worry about it! We have to keep running until we get home!"

They made it to the fun house, but there was no sign of Pete and Joseph. Had they had enough time to go all the way through? Were they on their way to the fried cake booth, or were they still inside? Sonny stopped someone coming out. "How long does it take to make it through the fun house?"

"Only a few minutes," the man said. "It's great though! You should do it!"

"What do you think?" he asked Constance.

"I don't know. We didn't ride the Ferris wheel. I'm not sure how long we were . . ." She stopped talking and shrugged her shoulders. He knew what she meant.

Sonny didn't know what to do. He looked at Connie. He knew he had to get her home. He took a deep breath and told her not to worry. Suddenly, they heard Pete laughing somewhere behind them.

Connie turned around. "Joseph! Joseph!" she screamed. She ran to him and tried to explain what had happened. Joseph hugged her tightly. She wasn't making sense. Confused, Joseph looked to Sonny for information.

"It was horrible!" Sonny said. "We have to get back to Aunt Sylvi. These guys are scary, Gordano! They pulled Connie up by her hair! Nearly lifted her off the ground! They threatened her, and you, and Aunt Sylvi. And look at her legs!"

Joseph let go of Connie and pushed her back a little. Her legs were cut and bleeding from the knees down. "What did they do to you?" His voice cracked a little.

Connie shook her head. "I fell. We need to go! Let's just go! I don't know where they went. I want to go and call Detective Rafferty!"

"Good idea." Joseph took her by the hand. "Be careful. Aunt Sylvi will get you cleaned up. I'll help. I promise. I won't let anything happen to you. I'm so sorry, Connie."

The four walked swiftly to their bikes. Pete talked with Sonny, who was visibly shaken by the ordeal, while Joseph supported Connie. Their bikes were covered with mud, but it didn't matter now. Once on their bikes, they pedaled as fast as they could to Aunt Sylvi's house. No one looked back. Connie's knees burned, but she didn't stop.

They finally reached Aunt Sylvi's and ditched their bikes in the yard. Joseph ran to the back porch and through the door while Pete and Sonny helped Connie.

"Aunt Sylvi! Aunt Sylvi! Help! We need help!" He ran to the kitchen. No Aunt Sylvi. "Aunt Sylvi! Where are you? It's an emergency!" He went to her bedroom and knocked on her door. "Aunt Sylvi?"

"I'm here, child!" Aunt Sylvi hurried down the stairs as fast as her thick, short legs would carry her. She was in her bathrobe. "I was tidying up a bit. What is it, child? Are you okay?" She took his face in her hands and looked at him.

He took her hand and shook his head. "No, it's not me!" Aunt Sylvi looked up as Connie came through the door with Pete and Sonny.

"Constance, dear!" She ran to Aunt Sylvi and burst into tears.

"What has happened, Joseph? Boys! What has happened?" She looked from Pete to Sonny. Sonny began to cry.

"We have to call Detective Rafferty right away!" Joseph pulled the card from his wallet and ran to the kitchen.

"You can tell me about this later, dear. Let's just get you cleaned up. Come into my bathroom, love. Are you hurt anywhere else?" Connie and Aunt Sylvi disappeared into her bathroom.

Pete put his arm around Sonny's shoulder, and they walked into the kitchen where Joseph was already on the telephone with the precinct. "Please tell him this is Joseph Gordano and this is an emergency. My family is in danger. I need him at my Aunt Sylvi's house right away. . . . Okay. . . . Yes, ma'am. . . . Thank you, ma'am. How long before you think you can reach him? . . . Okay. Thank you. . . . Yes, ma'am. We will." Joseph hung up and turned to his friends.

"They are sending over a patrol car," he explained. "The patrol man will take our information until they can reach Rafferty. They think Rafferty should be here within an hour or so. How's Connie?" He peered out of the kitchen toward Aunt Sylvi's bathroom. The door was still closed. *What is taking so long?* He turned around and sat down at the table with Pete and Sonny. "Are you okay?" he asked Sonny.

"I don't know, Joe. Really, I don't know." Sonny was trying to be strong. His eyes were red, and Joseph could see his hands shaking. "They pushed their way between us and held me back. I couldn't do anything." He buried his face in his hands. "I couldn't do anything. I could hear Connie crying out, and I couldn't do anything to rescue her."

"It's okay, Sonny!" Joseph got up and put a hand on Sonny's shoulder. "It's not your fault! It's Uncle Gordy's fault. It's all his fault. He stole Aunt Sylvi's jewelry. He did this to Connie and to you. And now he's put Aunt Sylvi and all of us in danger! I hope they put him in jail forever!"

"Joseph Gordano!" Aunt Sylvi helped Connie into the kitchen. "What is this all about?"

"I'm afraid it's true," Connie said, taking a seat at the table.

"I don't quite understand." Aunt Sylvi went to a tin box on the cabinet, took out a loaf of cinnamon bread, and sliced it on a plate. She brought it to the table.

"Aunt Sylvi, stop. Please sit down and listen." Joseph pulled a chair out and motioned for her to have a seat.

Flustered, she wiped her hands on a dish towel and sat down. Pete stood up and scooted his chair closer to her. Joseph looked at Pete, then sat down facing Aunt Sylvi. "Aunt Sylvi, Uncle Gordy has gotten involved with some bad men called the Barcolli brothers."

"Child!" Aunt Sylvi protested.

"It's true." Connie put her hand on Aunt Sylvi's.

"He owes them money, and we guess he must have stolen your jewelry to pay them," Joseph explained somberly.

"No! Now Joseph Gordano, of all things!" Aunt Sylvi stood. "I will not hear of such nonsense!"

"Maybe you will believe it if you hear it from Detective Rafferty. He is on his way over." Joseph stood as well.

"Why, dear?" she protested.

"The Barcollis want their money, and Uncle Gordy hasn't paid on time. They followed us at the carnival," Joseph continued.

"Who did, dear?"

"The Barcolli brothers," all four children quickly replied.

"Sakes!" Aunt Sylvi gasped.

"They cornered Sonny and Connie. They split them up. They held Connie by the hair and nearly lifted her off the ground, Aunt Sylvi!" Joseph said gravely. "They breathed in her face and threatened her. They threatened you and me, too, if Uncle Gordy doesn't pay them tomorrow."

"Goodness me, child!" Aunt Sylvi looked shocked. She turned to Connie, "It's no wonder you are shaking to the bone! Oh, my dears!" She reached over and touched Sonny's face. She paced around the kitchen, trying to let the news sink in. Had her own son really done this? Methodically, she pulled out four glasses from the cabinet. She took milk from the refrigerator, filled the glasses, and placed them on the table. "You say Detective Rafferty is on his way here?" she asked Joseph.

"He couldn't be reached at the time I called. They were certain they would be able to reach him within the hour. In the meantime, they are going to send over a patrol man. We are supposed to tell him everything."

"As soon as you boys talk to Detective Rafferty"—she looked at Pete and Sonny—"I want you to go straight home. Do you understand me?"

"Yes, ma'am," the boys replied.

"Sonny's staying over at my house, Aunt Sylvi," Pete explained. "His mom already knows."

"That's fine, son. That's just fine." Aunt Sylvi began to wander around the kitchen again. "I would like very much if you would call me when you get to your house, please."

There was a knock at the door.

"Yes, ma'am," Pete and Sonny answered as Sylvi left the kitchen.

"Now you all stay here," Aunt Sylvi directed.

"I'm coming with you," Joseph said.

At the door were two uniformed patrol officers. "Mrs. Gordano?" one of them asked. Aunt Sylvi nodded. "Detective Rafferty asked us to keep you company for a few minutes. He is on his way."

"Thank you, gentlemen." She stepped aside. "Won't you come in? I just sliced up some fresh cinnamon bread."

The officers stepped inside and removed their hats. "No thank you, ma'am," the first officer continued, "but that's a mighty nice offer. We'll just stay here until Detective Rafferty arrives."

"We were told to give you our statements," Joseph said.

"Yes, son. That was, in fact, the plan," the officer explained. "But Detective Rafferty insisted he be the one to take your statements. So we are here for safety purposes until he arrives."

Joseph went back into the kitchen. Sylvi took a moment and looked into each of the officers' eyes. She nodded to them, thanked them, then slowly and deliberately turned back to the kitchen.

Suddenly, Uncle Gordy appeared at the back door. Aunt Sylvi stopped and stared at him.

"What is it, Ma?" He looked from his mother to the police officers.

"Vincent Gordano?" the officer asked as he stepped farther into the entryway.

Gordy looked terrified. He had no idea what to do. Should he try to run? No, he couldn't let them shoot him in front of his mother. That's what they would do, right? Shoot him? He had never been in trouble with the law before. But he sure was in trouble now. Or was he? What *exactly* did they know?

"I know, son," his mother said to him. "We all know."

"What do you know?" Gordy wanted to play it cool.

"Vincent Gordano, the Barcolli brothers made threats against your family this evening. To keep your family as safe as possible, we would like you to leave the premises. You may return in the daylight hours. Do we have your cooperation?" the officer asked Gordy, but Gordy knew it wasn't an option.

Gordy put his hands in the air. "I'll be over at Nancy's, Ma."

"Disgrace!" Aunt Sylvi said and turned away with her hand over her mouth. She sank into the closest chair and began to sob. Sonny and Connie sat in miserable silence. Joseph and Pete leaned against the cabinet. All hung their heads low. There was no way to comfort Aunt Sylvi right now.

Rafferty appeared in the kitchen doorway and knocked on the wall as he entered. "Excuse me, folks. Mrs. Gordano, I understand Vincent has just left. I know it was hard, but I believe keeping him away from the house tonight is for the best."

Sylvi dabbed her face with the handkerchief she kept tucked in her bathrobe sleeve. "Yes, Detective. Thank you for your thoughtfulness. I agree it is best. I just cannot believe Vincent has done this. And these men that have threatened the children. My goodness!"

"Why don't we start there?" He looked around. "Who exactly was threatened?"

"Connie," the boys answered.

"I was," Connie said.

"Connie, would you mind coming out to the dining room with me to tell me what happened?"

"Okay. Can Joseph come with me?"

"I'm sorry, young lady. I need to hear from each of you individually."

"If I go first," Joseph interrupted, "then could I sit in with her when it's her turn?"

"Sure." Rafferty smiled. "Looks like that makes you first, son."

Joseph followed Detective Rafferty into the dining room where he told him about seeing Uncle Gordy and the Barcolli brothers at the carnival. He also told him about the other times before the carnival when he and Connie had seen the Barcollis. He confirmed that he had not actually seen them approach Connie and Sonny.

Detective Rafferty thanked him and asked him to stay put while he went and got Connie. When they returned, Rafferty took his seat, and Joseph moved to the next chair to give her the seat nearest Rafferty.

The interview began. "When did you first see the Barcolli brothers?

"Do you mean at the carnival or ever?" Connie questioned.

"We can start with ever. That will be fine." He took notes as she told the same story Joseph had, right up until they split up at the carnival.

"Now, take your time, Connie. I know this is difficult. But I need you to tell me exactly what they said and exactly what happened."

She nodded. Under the table she tapped Joseph's leg with her hand. He took it and gave an encouraging squeeze. Connie held back tears as she explained what happened in line at the Ferris wheel. She described the Barcolli brothers and told Rafferty what they had said.

Detective Rafferty asked if they had inflicted any physical wounds to her body. "Cuts, gashes, bruises, etc."

"No, not really." She rubbed the back of her head. "They lifted me from the ground by my hair, so my scalp is a little sore. That's all."

Rafferty smiled. "That counts." He glanced under the table. "I noticed your knees are all bandaged up. What happened there?"

"I fell while I was running to find Joseph after it happened," Connie explained as she glanced over at her friend.

"Is it bad enough to be seen by a doctor?" the detective inquired.

"It sure looked bad to me!" Joseph interrupted. "There was an awful lot of blood. It was running into her socks!"

"It's okay, really." Connie turned to him. "Aunt Sylvi said I had one big gash, but she put some tape on it. She said it was really strong tape that Mr. Gordano used to use for large cuts."

"Okay then," Detective Rafferty chuckled. "If you think of anything else you want to tell me, you can call me anytime." He slid another of his cards across the table to her.

"Thank you," Connie said as she took the card from him.

"Why don't you two have Sonny come on in?" Rafferty nodded his head toward the kitchen.

Joseph and Connie joined Aunt Sylvi and Pete while Sonny made his way into the dining room. When he returned to the kitchen, he motioned to Pete, who was leaning against the cabinet. Pete nodded and went in to take his turn.

The others sat quietly in the kitchen. Aunt Sylvi sat for moment and then moved about when the tears overtook her again.

Finally, Rafferty and Pete joined them. "I think I am finished with you young people. You all did a fine job. A fine job indeed."

Aunt Sylvi stood and gave her face one last dab with her handkerchief. "Okay now, boys, let's get you home."

"Where are you headed, fellas?" Detective Rafferty asked.

"Sonny is staying over at my house tonight. His mom already knows," Pete explained again.

"Ever take a ride in a patrol car?" Detective Rafferty grinned.

"No, sir." Pete and Sonny shook their heads with wide eyes.

Detective Rafferty leaned out of the kitchen to address one of the patrolmen in the entryway. "Officer Whitlock, would you kindly give these gentlemen a ride home? And please make sure their bicycles make the trip safely as well. Pete and Sonny, why don't you show him where your bikes are. Go ahead and say your goodbyes here."

Sonny walked over to Connie who was seated at the table. "Connie, I really hope you are okay. Pete and I will come back tomorrow." He smiled awkwardly.

"Sonny, I'm okay," Connie said and smiled back. "It will be nice to see you guys tomorrow." She stood and gave him a hug.

While Connie and Sonny finished saying goodbye, Pete hugged Aunt Sylvi and talked to Joseph. They agreed to get together tomorrow after lunch sometime. Sonny hugged Aunt Sylvi as well, and Pete gave Constance a squeeze. "I sure hope you can get some rest tonight, Connie. We'll see you tomorrow afternoon. Okay?" Pete said sweetly.

"Sure, Pete. Thanks. Tomorrow afternoon," Connie agreed.

Joseph walked his friends out to get their bikes. Officer Whitlock had moved his patrol car to the back alley. Truth was, Joseph was a little jealous. He had never ridden in a patrol car either. He supposed they wouldn't be allowed to turn on the sirens, but, gee, wouldn't that be swell?

He waved goodbye, locked the back door, and meandered into the kitchen. Connie's arms were folded on the table, and her head was resting on them. Aunt Sylvi and Detective Rafferty were still talking quietly. Connie looked up at Joseph. "Do you think we could sleep up in the attic tonight?"

"I don't know?" He shrugged his shoulders. "What do you think, Aunt Sylvi?"

"Well, it certainly is drafty. It's all right with me, dears, if you feel safer up there. But do be sure to use plenty of blankets."

"Wait. No!" Joseph changed his mind. "I don't like the idea of leaving you all the way down here alone, Aunt Sylvi."

"Actually," Detective Rafferty chimed in, "I believe this house needs a twenty-four-hour watch tonight. The Barcolli brothers are serious characters. I have no one who would miss me at home. So if you wouldn't mind, Sylvi, I would be honored to be your watchman for the night."

"Detective Rafferty! I couldn't ask you to do that! It's just too much!" she exclaimed, overwhelmed by his offer.

"Well, then." Detective Rafferty said thoughtfully. "How about in trade for a nice pot of coffee and a slice of that cinnamon bread I saw the boys eating? And please, call me Michael."

"Oh!" Aunt Sylvi blushed slightly. "Okay then, Michael. I'll slice up the rest of the loaf just for you!" She giggled. "Shall I make you up a bed on the sofa?"

"Actually, just a blanket and a pillow would be great. If I sleep, it will only be a cat nap. I have patrol cars stationed in front of the house and in the alley. They will rotate shifts throughout the night. If so much as a mouse tries to get in here, we will know about it."

Aunt Sylvi shivered. "Oh, I certainly hope so! Joseph knows how I hate the mice!"

"You probably should have used a different example!" Joseph laughed. "Now she won't just be awake worrying about the Barcollis; she'll be up thinking about mice too! She won't sleep a wink!" He kissed his aunt on the cheek and gave her a hug, then turned to Rafferty with an extended hand and smiled. "Thank you, sir."

Connie walked slowly from the kitchen to the doorway. She couldn't remember ever feeling this worn out. She turned slowly and gave a small wave. "Good night, everyone. Thanks for everything. Aunt Sylvi, do you think I could take a bubble bath in the morning?"

"Of course, my dear." Aunt Sylvi patted her cheek. "Get some rest now."

"Good night, young lady," Detective Rafferty said. "I'll be here all night if you need anything."

Connie nodded and followed Joseph up the stairs. They stopped in her bedroom. Joseph grabbed his sleeping bag and pillow, then waited in the hallway while Connie changed into her night clothes. She opened the door with a smile on her face. "I'm ready. Let's go."

Joseph was a little surprised. She seemed more like herself. "Does it feel good to have your night-gown on? Or Marie's nightgown, I should say," he teased.

"It does, actually. And it feels good to be done with all of the carnival drama too. Want to play some cards or something when we get upstairs?"

"Gee, Connie, I don't know." They turned to the attic. "I think maybe you should get some rest. You looked awful tired downstairs. What if we just talk?

If we can't sleep, then we'll play cards." He dropped his sleeping bag on the floor. "You sleep on the sofa." He went to the box where he had found the quilt a few days before and grabbed a couple of blankets.

Connie helped him get set up on the floor, and before long they turned off the light and settled down to sleep. "Wow," she said softly. "It's so bright up here. Look, Joseph. Look out that window over there. It's a full moon. No wonder it's so bright. I remember I looked out the window over my bed at Grandpa's the night before I came here. The moon looked just like that. Crazy!"

"What's your school like?" Joseph had been wondering more and more about her life in the future.

"I'll be starting a new one next year. So, I don't know," Connie replied.

"I just wonder if it's much different from mine."

"I doubt it." She was nervous about her new school and didn't really want to talk about it.

"You are probably right." Joseph sighed. "School is school, I guess."

"Hey . . ." She rolled over and looked down at him. "What's with all the comic books in your room? You never read them or even talk about them. You must have hundreds of them."

"Uncle Gordy gave those to me last summer. It is his old collection. He wanted me to have it. Said it would be worth a lot of money someday."

"Maybe he should have thought of selling those instead of his mother's jewelry," Connie declared.

"I don't know what he was thinking," Joseph grumbled, slightly frustrated that they were talking about it again. "Let's just get some sleep."

"Okay, Joseph. You know, I wish you were my brother and you could go back home with me. Do you think I'll ever get home?"

"I don't know, Connie. I'm really sorry. I just don't know," Joseph whispered as he drifted off to sleep.

CHAPTER 9

The Chase

It was early, but Connie couldn't get back to sleep. She went downstairs to get some day clothes and see about having that bubble bath. Aunt Sylvi and Detective Rafferty were sitting at the breakfast table talking. She could smell the coffee. She wondered when Gordy would be home. What would happen then?

She stopped in the bathroom to brush her teeth, then started down the big staircase. She paused halfway down the stairs and looked back. It felt strange to be there without Joseph. Maybe she should have woken him up. Just as she considered going back, Aunt Sylvi called out to her.

"Good morning, dear! You are up early! How are you feeling this morning?"

Connie entered the kitchen and gave Aunt Sylvi a hug. "Good morning, Aunt Sylvi. Good morning, Detective Rafferty. I'm doing just fine, I think. Thank you." She took a seat at the table. "Joseph is still sleeping. I was just thinking about going back up to get him."

"Don't have to!" Joseph popped into the kitchen. Aunt Sylvi and Connie both jumped in fright.

"Joseph Gordano!" his aunt addressed him sternly. "Now is not the time for foolishness! You have startled us!"

Joseph chuckled. "Gosh. I'm sorry. I didn't mean to." He kissed Aunt Sylvi's cheek. "Good morning, Detective." He walked over to Connie and squeezed her shoulder. "Good morning, Connie. How are your arms this morning, tough guy?"

"Joseph!" Aunt Sylvi gasped and Connie giggled.

"I'm actually pretty sore. Looking forward to that bubble bath though!" Connie replied.

"Connie here took three swings at the strong man machine last night," Joseph explained. "You know, the one with the big sledgehammer thing?"

"Those are mighty heavy, young lady!" Detective Rafferty said. "You should be careful fooling around like that."

"Oh, she wasn't fooling around! She was steaming mad is what she was! Connie lifted that hammer completely over her head!" Joseph demonstrated.

"You are kidding?" Detective Rafferty looked at Connie in amazement. "Not to insult you, Connie, but you are a girl of small stature. I know men who can't do that."

"Well, sir, I think it was my anger working, not me!" she admitted with a grin.

"Connie lifted it over her head not once! Not twice! But three times! And on the third time she hit the bell! Ding!" Joseph bragged.

"You don't say?" Detective Rafferty was nearly speechless.

"She won a little pair of gold boxing gloves to prove it. What did you do with them, Connie?" Joseph asked.

"I forgot all about those. I had Sonny carry them. He put them in his pocket."

"We have about twenty minutes until breakfast is ready," Aunt Sylvi interrupted. "Connie, why don't you go ahead and get your bath. Joseph, you can set the table.

"Gee, thanks!" He laughed.

Aunt Sylvi gently tapped his mouth. "Don't sass. Now Connie, why don't you use my bathtub? My good bubbles are down here." She took her into her bathroom and was back within a few minutes. She proceeded to prepare the meal.

In the bathroom, Connie let the water run as far up to the top of the tub as she could. Aunt Sylvi's tub was huge, and Connie loved soaking in it. She sank down into the warm scented bubbles and began to pray and thank God for keeping her safe. As she prayed, she drifted off to sleep. She was completely relaxed.

While she soaked, Joseph made the best of his table setting duties. He had enjoyed watching Connie pick the tablecloths and dishes. This morning, he picked a white lace tablecloth and the pink dishes. He thought she would like those.

"Joseph, darling! Would you please go knock on the door and tell Constance that breakfast is ready?" Aunt Sylvi called to him from the kitchen.

"Sure, Aunt Sylvi." He ran to the bathroom and startled her with a knock. "Come eat!" he said. There was no answer. "Connie! Breakfast!"

"Blub-bleh-okay, thanks!" Connie sputtered. "I'll be right out!" She had gradually sunk deeper into the tub. Her mouth was totally beneath the water line when Joseph knocked.

Once they were all at the dining room table, Detective Rafferty asked what had angered Connie so badly at the carnival the previous evening. Joseph laughed and they proceeded to tell both him and Aunt Sylvi about the fun times they had, including the Menagerie of Oddities and the games. However, they were disappointed that they did not get to ride any of the rides. They discussed whether they would feel comfortable going back tonight. Rafferty told them he would rather them wait a few days. The carnival would be in town another week.

"After breakfast, we'd better clean the mud off the bikes. Okay?" Joseph said to Connie.

"Sure. That sounds good," she agreed. A silence fell as they finished their food. Connie and Joseph were dying to talk more about Uncle Gordy, but they knew it was not a good idea in front of Aunt

Sylvi. Instead, Joseph asked Detective Rafferty about the patrol cars.

Detective Rafferty told them that the patrol cars had left at sunup, but there would be cars on patrol regularly in the area. He explained that he, too, would have to leave soon. He needed to go home and get cleaned up so he could head to the precinct. If they needed him, they were to call him there.

As far as cleaning off their bikes, Rafferty suggested they wash them right away in the yard while he was still there. If they wanted to dry them off or do any other kind of work on them, they should probably do that in the garage away from the windows.

"Otherwise, stay in the house as much as you can today," he told them. "We have guys watching the Barcolli brothers right now. They should not be a problem. If you hear from Vincent, please give me a call. I would like you to keep me posted. Now you kids better get to washing those bikes."

"Yes, sir," Joseph answered as they jumped up from the table.

"The washing buckets are in the laundry area, dear." Aunt Sylvi informed as they left the kitchen.

Joseph and Connie began filling buckets and rinsing the mud from the bicycles. They were nearly done when Detective Rafferty came out on the back porch. "How is it going out here? Almost finished?"

"We sure are, sir," Joseph answered.

"Do you think you can go ahead and finish up?" he asked. "I need to be going."

"Yes, sir," they replied.

While they finished, Detective Rafferty walked around the yard, looked up and down the alley, and went into the garage for a moment. When he came out, he was rubbing some of the thick white dust and pebbles between his fingers. "You kids know what this white dust is?"

Connie looked up. "No, sir. But I find it highly suspicious. I am determined to get to the bottom of it, sir."

"Good job, Officer Constance," Detective Rafferty said proudly. That made her giggle. "I want a full report upon my return."

She stood up straight and gave him a salute. "Yes, sir."

"Okay, kids. Let's get those bikes in the garage," Detective Rafferty directed.

"We're ready," Joseph said. "If only someone would quit clowning around!"

"I'll see you later!" Rafferty smiled as he walked back to the house.

Joseph took the bikes to the far corner of the garage behind Aunt Sylvi's big yellow car. They took a few minutes collecting rags from the rag buckets and various towels that were stashed around the garage. They had rushed the rinse a little since the detective had to leave. They needed to work fast to wipe away the remaining mud before it dried again.

They were working diligently when they heard voices. Connie and Joseph looked at each other and then crouched down. From under Aunt Sylvi's car, they watched the garage door open.

"You won't believe it. They have been in here all along," Uncle Gordy bragged. Connie raised her eyebrows at Joseph.

"Oh, Vinnie, you are so smart!" It was Nancy. "Heh heh heh heh heh heh," she chipmunk-laughed. They had barely entered the doorway when they stopped and turned around.

Connie crept up to peer through the window of Aunt Sylvi's car. Joseph tried to pull her down, but once she shrugged him off, he joined her. They watched Uncle Gordy remove a concrete block from above the doorway. White dust and pebbles fell to the floor. Gordy reached into the hole where the block had been and pulled out something white that looked like an old T-shirt. He turned to the work bench, unwrapped it, and uncovered Aunt Sylvi's jewelry.

"Oh, Vinnie! They are gorgeous! Are you sure I can't just have something?" Nancy whined.

"Are you crazy? These are my mother's!" Uncle Gordy replied harshly. "I'm meeting old man Smithers at his shop today at ten o'clock. Says he'll give me the cash. Then I can finally get the Barcollis off my back once and for all."

Gordy rewrapped the jewelry, reached up, and shoved the bundle back into its hiding place. Once it was secure, he returned the concrete block.

"Let's go get some breakfast. We have a couple of hours before we meet Smithers," Uncle Gordy said as he glanced at his watch. "I don't want to stick around here." He closed the door and disappeared down the alley.

Connie sat down and exhaled. "Oh my goodness, Joseph! What do we do?"

"I don't know. I need to think a minute." Joseph rested his head as he hugged his knees. After a moment he looked at her and said, "Let's go."

"Where are we going?" Connie asked. She was shaking a little and it scared her. *Deep breath!*

"Just follow me. We are taking back Aunt Sylvi's jewelry first! That's for sure!" Joseph said firmly.

Another deep breath. "All right! Let's do it!" Connie was ready for a fight.

They searched for a ladder, not too tall but tall enough to reach the jewelry. Finally, they settled on a step stool. It was tall enough to reach the concrete block, but Joseph could not seem to get it out.

"Look for a hole or a rim or something to grab on to," Connie suggested.

"I am," Joseph replied. "It's almost flat. Wait . . . there's nothing!"

"Well, Gordy got it out somehow!" she argued.

"Maybe he has bigger hands than me!" Joseph shot back.

"That certainly is a possibility considering you are twelve and he is . . . not!" Connie was getting frustrated. What if he came back?

"Okay, Miss Know-It-All, you try!" Joseph came down from the stool and steadied it for Connie.

"Thank you. I will!" she snipped.

She, too, ran into the same problems as Joseph. "Okay, you're right." Connie admitted reluctantly. "We don't have time for you to rub it in. Let's figure something out." She looked around. "Say, does Aunt Sylvi keep any of the sticky tape she used on my knee out here?"

"I'm sure she does. She uses it on everything." Joseph began to search the garage. "Here, I've got some." He waved it victoriously.

Connie took the tape and tore off two long pieces. She took each piece and folded it over backward with the sticky side out. She sealed it against itself and made two big sticky circles. Carefully, she climbed the step stool and placed the circles on the concrete block. She pressed them down tightly. "Let's hope this works." Gently, she pulled on the tape. Slowly and surely, the concrete block moved. "Woo-hoo!" White dust and pebbles rained down on them as she dragged the heavy block from its place.

"I'm not sure I can reach up in here." Connie looked down at Joseph with concern.

"You have to, Connie. Come on! Reach! Stretch! You can do it!" he encouraged.

"But my arms hurt!" Connie complained as she stretched with all her might on her tiptoes. She lifted one leg to give her more reach. Her arm scraped against the concrete. She felt wobbly like she might fall, when at last she felt the soft T-shirt with her fingertips. "I can feel it! I can feel it! Oh my goodness!" She reached a little farther until she lost her balance and tumbled to the floor.

"Connie!" Joseph yelled. Somehow, he thought he might catch her. Instead, he just broke her fall.

"Are you okay?" they asked in unison.

"I'm fine," they both answered and laughed. It was then that Joseph spied the wadded white shirt next to Connie.

"Connie! Connie!" He scrambled to reach for it. "You did it! Here they are! You did it!" Joseph grabbed the shirt and sat upright. Slowly, he opened it. "This is it! Look! Uncle Sal's diamonds and my great-grandmother's pearls. It's all here!"

"What do we do now?" Constance asked as she wiped all the dust from her clothes.

"That is as far as I got." Joseph looked at her, perplexed.

She stared at him in silence for a moment. They had to have a plan. "Okay, we take them up to the attic and hide them. Let's take them out of the shirt and put them in something else." Connie thought for a moment. "An evidence bag! Yeah, an evidence bag. Then we call Detective Rafferty and tell him that Gordy is planning to take the jewelry to Mr. Smithers at ten o'clock. We'll tell Rafferty that we have the jewelry, so he will need to be here before ten. Once he gets here, we'll give him the jewelry and let him take it from there."

"Gee, that's a swell plan, Connie! Let's get out of here!" They ran inside as fast as they could. Their first concern was to let Aunt Sylvi know what was going on.

Joseph explained that he believed Uncle Gordy would be returning to the house soon. He told Aunt Sylvi that he planned to call Detective Rafferty and ask him to return in about an hour. "Aunt Sylvi, the detective should be here ready and waiting for Uncle Gordy. Connie and I are going to stand watch in the attic." They didn't tell her they had the jewelry. "Do you want to wait up there with us?"

"No, dearest." She sighed heavily. "I'll need to be here in case Detective Rafferty needs me. I do think I'll just wait in my room. Joseph, you be sure to lock the attic door. Vincent knows you two have made your club house up there."

"We will be okay, Aunt Sylvi. Don't worry," Joseph assured her. "But you should probably go ahead and get settled in your room."

"Oh, sakes. Such a rush!" Aunt Sylvi replied. "But you are right, Joseph. You are absolutely right. We must all be safe. I'll get a book and my quilt and try not to worry." Her anxiety was apparent. "I'll leave my door open until I hear you two go upstairs. Now, be careful. Hurry up, and don't forget to lock the door." She gave them each a kiss on the head and disappeared into her room.

Joseph quickly telephoned the precinct. "Detective Rafferty, please. . . . Yes, ma'am. Joseph Gordano. . . . Yes, ma'am. . . . Okay. Okay. Thank you. . . . Yes. He is coming back at ten o'clock. Please tell Detective Rafferty to be here as soon as he can. . . . Thank you, ma'am. Goodbye."

"She was actually expecting our call," Joseph told Connie. "Rafferty isn't in yet, but she will pass the message on to him. He'll be here before Uncle Gordy. Let's get ready." He motioned toward the stairs.

"How about some reinforcements for the stake-out?" Connie motioned to the kitchen and smiled.

"I must be rubbing off on you!" Joseph laughed as he led the way to raid the refrigerator. There was nothing there that interested them, so they moved on to the cabinets and pantry. Joseph found some chocolate bars and lemon cookies. Connie found two apples and some crackers. They each decided to take a glass of milk. Carefully, they balanced their snack stash as they ran up to the attic.

After they unloaded their food, Connie took the jewelry and slid it into an evidence bag. She marked it with a star and stuffed it in one of the old cardboard boxes that was stacked in the corner.

Now it was time to wait. Connie was the lookout for Detective Rafferty, and Joseph was the lookout for Uncle Gordy. They had plenty of time to pull chairs over to the windows, set the snacks on a table between them, and get out Grandpa's binoculars. She called dibs on the spinning chair.

Since Uncle Gordy was leaving at 10:00, they hoped the detective would arrive by 9:40 at the latest. They set themselves a deadline of 9:30, which was when they would stop snacking and chatting and get serious about the lookout.

At 9:30 on the dot, Connie announced, "It's time. Let's do it!" She got out the binoculars, stopped spinning, and put her focus on the street below. "Detective Rafferty should be here soon." They continued to sit for several minutes. They waited. They watched. "Joseph," she said slowly without lowering the binoculars, "I just had a really bad feeling."

"What's that?" he asked as he watched Aunt Sylvi's backyard.

"Did Gordy say he was *leaving* at ten o'clock to meet Mr. Smithers, or that his *appointment* was at ten o'clock?" She turned to look at Joseph.

Joseph began to breathe heavily. "Holy cow, Connie. I don't know."

"Never mind! Thank goodness! I can see Detective Rafferty's car! We're okay. He's coming, Joseph! He's coming!"

"Connie . . ." Joseph felt like he was going to faint. "Uncle Gordy just walked into the backyard. How close is Detective Rafferty?"

"He's at the stop sign at the corner! Oh, don't stop!" Constance cried, wishing the detective could hear her. "Come on! Come on!"

"He's going into the garage! Connie, where's Detective Rafferty?" Joseph began to panic.

Uncle Gordy stepped out of the garage and looked up at the attic window. He pointed a finger at Joseph. His face was full of rage.

"Here he comes, Connie! We have to hide *now*! Hide! Hide!"

Connie and Joseph scrambled for the cardboard boxes stacked on the opposite side of the room. They huddled behind them as quietly as they could and waited for Uncle Gordy. Heavy footsteps pounded up the stairs and got louder until he finally broke through the attic door.

"Come on, Joey!" Gordy pleaded in a desperate yet eerie voice. "Do you want to get me killed? You can't mess with me like this! You have no idea what you are getting into! Be a pal here, kid. Help me out."

There was silence. They could hear Uncle Gordy as he walked about. He got closer. Closer. Connie could see him through a small crack in the boxes. She motioned to Joseph to push the boxes over. He nodded. She held up one finger, then two, then three, then a fist. In one swift movement, she and Joseph shoved a tower of boxes over on Uncle Gordy.

They rushed past him as he struggled to his feet. They raced down the steps and around the corner. Joseph took Connie's hand and they ran down the hall. Uncle Gordy was gaining on them, and Joseph was about to pull Connie's arm right out of its socket. Just when she thought she couldn't run any faster, Joseph ducked into the hall closet. They could hear Detective Rafferty come in the front door downstairs. Joseph secured the closet door, and Connie scooted as far to the back of the closet as she could. She leaned back against the wall.

"Aaaaaahhhhhhhhh!" Connie fell backward through the closet wall. She tumbled and tumbled until she landed with a thud on the hardwood floor.

CHAPTER 10

Joseph!

"Joseph?" Connie whispered frantically. "Joseph!" He did not reply. There was only silence. She could not hear Uncle Gordy. She could not hear Rafferty. She couldn't hear anything. She fumbled to the door, getting tangled in a pile of boots and shoes. Slowly she opened the door and peered cautiously around the corner.

"Wait a minute!" Connie cried and threw the door open. She was back in her bedroom at her grandpa's house. Her heart raced. Her legs wobbled beneath her. She fell on the bed and let out a sigh. "That was so crazy!"

She lay there a few seconds before she sat straight back up. *Joseph! Where was he? What happened? Uncle Gordy? Detective Rafferty? Oh no!*

She rushed down the stairs and into the kitchen. She bumped smack-dab into Anthony in the hall. "Watch it, squirt," he muttered as he balanced a stack of cookies on a napkin.

Constance said something in reply and went in search of the old phone book Grandpa always kept around. "Gandy, Gardner, Gither,

Gizzard . . . *Gizzard?* Poor guy. Gordano! Joseph Gordano, 325 North Chestnut, Frontenac." She scribbled the address down, stuck it in her pocket, and hurried out the door. She could tell it had been raining, but the sun was out now. There was probably a rainbow somewhere, but she had no time to look.

"Ouch! Crazy helmet," Connie grumbled as she pinched herself with the strap. She mounted her bike just as Aunt Jen pulled into the driveway.

"Hi, honey!" Aunt Jen called.

"Hi. I'll be home for dinner!" Connie called over her shoulder. She pedaled away before Aunt Jen could protest.

Connie had no idea where she was going, but she knew they passed a sign to Frontenac on their way from Kansas City, so that was the direction she headed. She pedaled as fast as she could. Her knees began to burn. Eventually, she slowed to a coast and stopped at a gas station for directions.

When she got off her bike she could barely walk. *Ding!* The gas station door alerted her entrance. "You need some help?" the nearly toothless man behind the counter asked.

"Yes, please. Am I in Frontenac yet?"

"Sure are. Where are you headed?" The man leaned forward on his elbows.

"Three two five North Chestnut," Connie answered.

"The road out front is Elm. The road out back is Maple." He gestured with one hand. "If you go one more road past Maple, that's Chestnut. You will want to take a left there. That is the good news. Bad news is you have about another mile and a half to go once you hit Chestnut."

"A mile and a half?" Connie groaned. "How many blocks is that?"

The man laughed. "Just keep going down Chestnut until you see a field on your left. Number three twenty-five should be just up the road there on your right. Big yellow house, I believe."

"Thank you, sir!" Connie called over her shoulder as she opened the door.

Ding! The door answered back.

Back on the bike, she turned left on Chestnut and looked for a field. She thought she would never find it. "Finally, there it is!" She saw it coming up on the left and began to pedal slower. She started to feel nervous. What if it wasn't him? What if it *was*? Had he gotten away from Uncle Gordy?

"Crazy!" she whispered as she slammed on her brakes.

There it was. A big yellow house with a small porch and white shutters. Could it be? Connie jumped off her bike and slowly walked it up the gravel driveway. She lowered the kickstand, parked it at the bottom of the steps, and made her way to a big screen door.

As she knocked nervously, she thought, *Could I have dreamed all of this? What if I spelled his name wrong? Maybe I should just go home.* The door opened.

On the other side of the screen stood a girl about Connie's age. "Hi," she said.

"Um, hi! Um … I'm looking for Joseph Gordano?" Connie stammered.

"That's my grandpa. He's not here right now, but he'll be right back. Want to wait?" the girl asked as she held the door open.

"Ah, sure, I guess." Connie slowly entered the house. They stood awkwardly and stared at each other for a moment inside the door until the girl said, "Sorry, I guess I should ask you if you want to sit down or something."

"That's okay," Connie said. She looked around the room for some kind of clue that this girl's grandpa was her friend Joseph, but nothing seemed familiar. Nothing looked like it might have belonged to Aunt Sylvi either. She had a sinking feeling deep in her stomach. The reality of the last four days began to hit her, or could she even call it *reality*? She missed her friend Joseph.

"Want a Popsicle?" the girl asked as she walked to the kitchen.

"Sure, I guess, thanks," Connie replied. "I'll have an orange one, please." She followed her in a daze. *Where are you, Joseph? I need a picture or something!*

The girl reached up to open the freezer. "Sorry, all we have is red and purple. Grandpa always eats the orange ones first."

"What?" Connie suddenly snapped back from her daze. Had she just heard her correctly?

"I know. He's weird like that," the girl chuckled. "So, red or purple?"

"Sorry. I'll have purple. Thanks." Connie started to smile. A sense of relief came over her. But he was older now. This was all so crazy! Would Joseph remember her?

As the girl put the box back in the freezer, she went on. "Purple is my favorite. I like everything purple."

"Huh?" Connie asked. "I'm sorry, did you say something?" *What happened this morning? Is Joseph hurt? What happened to Uncle Gordy?*

"I'm Sydney, by the way." The girl interrupted Connie's thoughts. "We just moved in with my grandpa this summer. Let's go wait for him on the porch. What grade are you in? I'll be in fifth grade."

Connie's head started to spin. On the way to the porch, Sydney's mom walked through with a laundry basket.

"Well, hi!" she said, startled. "Syd, I didn't know you had company."

"I don't really." She pointed her Popsicle at Connie. "She's waiting for Grandpa. Her name is . . ." Sydney stopped. She realized she didn't even know the girl's name.

"Constance. My name is Constance. It's nice to meet you," she said in passing as the screen door closed behind them.

"Constance?" Sydney's mother whispered as her eyes grew wide. "Connie?" She dropped the laundry basket and watched the girls from the window. "It . . . couldn't . . . be." She slowly shook her head in disbelief.

"So, how do you know Grandpa?" Sydney asked as the girls sat down on the steps.

"Well . . ." Connie took a deep breath and wondered how much to share. "It's kind of crazy, but I have this closet—"

"Closet?" Sydney interrupted. "Oh my gosh! Mom!" Sydney yelled. "Mom!"

Connie grew nervous. What did she say? Should she go? Had she done something wrong? Before she knew it, Sydney's mom stood on the porch behind them.

"Mom!" Sydney cried again and jumped to her feet. "This is Crazy Connie! You're Crazy Connie, aren't you?" She was hopping up and down with excitement.

"What?" Connie said, confused. She began to panic. What should she do? "I'm *not* crazy!" she insisted. "Maybe I should go!"

"No, dear!" Sydney's mom reached out to her as Connie headed down the steps. "You don't understand. It's okay. Please, stay."

Connie stopped and looked back at Sydney and her mom. They both stood on the porch with strange smiles on their faces. *Maybe they are crazy!* Connie thought.

"Come with us." Sydney's mom motioned for her to follow. "Please, it's okay. I promise." Sydney smiled at her mom and took her hand. They then disappeared around the side of the house. Connie hurried to catch up. She followed them reluctantly to a staircase on the outside of the house that led to a small porch past the second story. Sydney's mom opened the door and motioned for the girls to go in.

Connie never expected what she saw. Inside, it looked like a log cabin. It was a beautiful office lined with bookshelves. Against one wall was a big wooden desk. All the lamps had colored glass lamp shades, and the walls were covered with black-and-white photographs. Connie noticed an especially large one across the room. It was different from the rest. It looked like it was made from a bunch of small photographs.

"This is Grandpa's office. He converted the attic. Isn't this awesome? He calls it his clubhouse," Sydney explained.

Connie smiled. Sydney's mom took her hand and led her to one of the tall bookshelves. She selected a book and handed it to Connie. "What is this?" She slowly reached for the book.

"*Crazy Connie's Closet*," she read the title out aloud. "Crazy Connie's Closet?" Connie repeated and looked up at Sydney, then at Sydney's mom.

She ran her fingers gently over her name as it appeared on the cover and then slowly opened the book. There on the first page were the words:

Dedicated to my dear friend Constance and the summer of 1959.

It was the best adventure of my life.

Connie's jaw dropped as the color drained from her face. She looked up at Sydney's mother, who gave her a gentle nod.

Connie stood there and stared at the book for what seemed like an hour. Suddenly, she noticed the familiar black-and-gold tassel. She turned to the page it marked. Attached to the tassel was the old, yellowed bookmark from Teeco's Tremendous that Joseph had just won at the carnival *last night*. She laughed.

"What are you laughing at?" a man asked from behind her.

She turned to see the tall man who stood in the doorway. *Could it be?* They stared at each other for a moment.

Finally, Joseph asked, "Been on any adventures lately?"

Connie gasped. She was absolutely filled with excitement. "Are you crazy? I just left your house this morning!" She ran and gave him a hug. "I'm so glad you are okay! I fell through right as Uncle Gordy was chasing us! What happened? You have to tell me everything!"

"Well, first of all, I see you have met my grand-daughter, Sydney, and my daughter, Kate. She's named after her mother, you know."

"No way!" Connie turned and looked at Kate, then back at Joseph. "You married Katherine Rose O'Malley?"

"I did."

"Holy cow!" She looked at Kate again. "This probably sounds crazy coming from a kid, but your dad knew he was going to marry your mother before he was twelve. I think that's so romantic!"

"Isn't it?" Kate smiled as she put her arm around her father. "Uncle Pete and Uncle Sonny tell me that same story."

"Ha! *Uncle Pete* and *Uncle Sonny*. That sounds so weird! So, Joseph, tell me what happened!" Connie wanted to know about Uncle Gordy and what happened to Aunt Sylvi's jewelry.

"Let's have a seat over here." He turned to his daughter and Sydney. "Would you ladies mind giving us some time to catch up? Oh, and Katie, would you mind bringing Connie up a Band-Aid? It looks like she needs a new one."

"Sure, Pop." Kate and Sydney left the office. The bike ride must have caused the cut on Connie's knee to start bleeding again. Kate was back quickly with a large bandage and some medical wipes. Joseph began carefully removing the old one first. "Ah, Uncle Sal's special tape. I haven't seen this in years. I'm actually going to leave that on for now. You know, you shouldn't remove that until the cut is healed." He cleaned it up and replaced the new bandage.

"Thanks. Done like a real grandpa." Connie smiled.

"Pretty strange, huh?" He leaned back in his chair and laughed and then got silent for a moment. Connie could tell he was remembering.

"Detective Rafferty came up the stairs just as Uncle Gordy was trying to open the closet. I didn't even know you were gone. They arrested Gordy for stealing the jewelry. It wasn't until Rafferty told us to come out that I realized you weren't there. I had to lie and tell him you weren't with me. Gordy thought he was losing his mind. He went to prison for a year; that was all. Aunt Sylvi made him move out. Rafferty was still concerned about the debt he owed the Barcolli brothers, even though Uncle Gordy was in jail. So Aunt Sylvi sold Gordy's motorcycle and some of the comic books he had given me. Turns out he hadn't really given them to me anyway. He just wanted to hide them in my room." Joseph sighed and shook his head.

"It was all very hard on Aunt Sylvi," Joseph continued. "Her son was going to jail, and you were gone. It was a very tough day for both of us. I had no idea I would miss you so much."

"Wow, you grew up to be so nice," Connie teased.

"Amazing, isn't it?" They laughed. "I still miss you! No girl I ever knew could make me laugh like you could. It's just so good to see you!" He paused for a minute and smiled at her. How wonderful it was to see his old friend.

"I have a great idea!" He stood. "Come over here with me." Connie followed him to the other side of the room and sat across the desk from him. He picked up the telephone. "Hang on just a second. I want to make a couple of phone calls." He had a very big smile on his face.

He put the phone to his ear and dialed. "Hey!" he said to someone on the other end. "You will never guess who I am sitting here looking at. . . . Ah, come on and guess. . . . You're no fun. Can I give you some hints? . . . Oh, lighten up. It's someone we've been waiting to hear from for almost *fifty* years." Joseph's expression changed a little. He stopped talking and listened. He noticed Connie was a little uncomfortable, so he shot her a smile and held up one finger. He turned his chair around so he wasn't facing her directly. "Eleven. The carnival was just a few days ago. . . . Okay, hang on." He turned back around with a smile on his face and dialed another number.

"Hi, Peg, it's Joe. Is our boy in the studio today? . . . Sure, thanks." Connie guessed he was on hold. He smiled again. "Hello! How are you, old man? . . . . I'm well, very well! I have a special guest today who we have been waiting for, and I think you will be surprised! I have Sonny on the other line. Hang on, I'm going to do a three-way call and put you both on the speaker. Are you ready? Okay, hang on. I think I know how to do this." He pressed some buttons on the phone and looked up at Connie. She could tell he was excited. Now that she realized what he was doing, she was excited too!

"Are you there?" he asked Sonny. "Okay, Pete is on the other line. Here we go. I love technology!"

"Are you guys there?" Joseph asked.

"I'm here," Connie heard one man answer.

"I'm here too. Hello?" the other man responded.

Connie was overwhelmed. She couldn't speak. She was sitting across from her dear friend, Joseph. He was safe. On the phone were the two men who had been with her through the most amazing experience of her life. They were grown now. And they had thought about her too. Waited for her. Joseph looked at her, expecting her to say something. Instead, she looked at him and tears streamed down her face.

"Connie? Are you there? It's Sonny." There was silence. "Joe? Pete? Anyone?"

"I'm still here," Pete said.

"We're still here," Joseph confirmed. "Maybe I should have given her a heads-up. I didn't tell her I was calling you guys."

"What's wrong?" Sonny asked.

Connie wiped her eyes and shook her head. She didn't want Joseph to say anything. "Just give us a second," Joseph told the guys. "Are you okay, Connie? What is it?"

She started to cry again. "I just came here so worried about you. Then I see you. And I hear you talk to Sonny and Pete about me. And now I find out you knew I would come one day. You guys are all grown up, but you still think about me. I just never would have imagined." She shrugged helplessly.

"Ah, honey!" Sonny said. "We've never stopped thinking about you."

"We have always considered you part of our gang." Pete laughed. "We kept you with us even when you weren't here!"

"Joe! Please give that girl a hug!" Sonny yelled.

Joseph got up and walked around to Connie. He knelt in front of her and held her as she cried.

"Okay! Now snap out of it!" Pete cried. "Because I really want to talk to you and see how you are!"

Connie laughed. "Hang on. Let me wipe my snot on Joseph's shirt." She took a tissue from the box on his desk and blew her nose. "Okay. I'm better now."

"That's our girl!" Pete laughed.

"Tell me you didn't!" Sonny said.

"You'll never know!" Connie laughed, feeling suddenly giddy.

"So how have you been, Connie? Fill us in with what's happened to you since we saw you last!" Pete said.

"That's hilarious. I saw you guys last night! Last I know, Joseph and I were chased by Uncle Gordy after we stole Aunt Sylvi's jewelry back this morning. I fell through the closet before Detective Rafferty got there, and I didn't know what happened to Joseph! That's why I'm here. I got on my bike and came to find him. Question is, what's happened with you guys all these years?"

Pete spoke again. "I'm still in St. Louis. I have actually done pretty well with photography, believe it or not. It all started with that old Polaroid camera my Uncle Jim gave me. Did Joseph show you the picture of us in his office?"

"No! Which one is it?" Connie asked, looking around the room. "I'm in the office now."

"The big one on the far wall. It's a collage."

"Cool. I'll be sure to look at it. What about you, Sonny? What are you up to? Are you in St Louis too?"

"Hi, sweetheart. It's good to hear your voice. Yes, I am in St. Louis. I'm a pediatrician."

"Wow. That's cool." Connie couldn't believe it. It was so weird that they were really grown up, with actual jobs.

"That's not the half of it," Pete interrupted. "Sonny also runs a clinic for abused children. He has dedicated his life to it. We're all incredibly proud of him."

"Yeah, and you thought *I* grew up to be nice!" Joseph teased Connie. "You should hear about all the stuff Sonny has done. He's just downright ridiculous!"

Sonny laughed. "Connie, honey, there must be a mistake. Who told you that Joseph grew up to be nice?" Everyone laughed. Just like yesterday—a lifetime ago.

"We have to get together!" Pete suggested. "Joseph, maybe you could bring Connie up to

St. Louis for the weekend sometime, now that she knows where you are."

"Sure, that would be great!" Constance said sarcastically. "Just as soon as I explain to my mom why I want to spend the weekend with three sixty-year-old men. That will go over really well!"

"Actually, I think it might be easier to explain than you think!" Joseph said. "Listen, guys. I need to talk to Connie about something. I'll be sure to get her contact information and send it to you both. We need to be getting off the phone now."

"It's been great talking with you, Connie! I'll be seeing you!" Pete said. "Take care."

"Goodbye, Pete."

There was silence for a moment until Joseph finally said, "Sonny, are you still there?"

"I'm here. Connie, please take care of yourself. Get my phone number from Joseph, okay? Call me if you need anything. Now that you know where we are, just know that I am always here for you."

"Thanks, Sonny. I promise I'll keep in touch."

"All right, pal, we'll talk with you later," Joseph said. "Goodbye."

"Wow, that was incredible. Thank you." Connie smiled at him.

"You're welcome." Joseph opened his middle desk drawer and took out a key. He walked over to one of his bookshelves that contained a small, locked cabinet. He unlocked it and took out an envelope.

"Come sit here where it's more comfortable." He pointed to the sofa.

Connie got up and switched seats. "What's up?" It all looked very mysterious.

"I want to tell you a story," Joseph began. "Did I ever tell you about my Uncle Joe?" Connie shook her head. "He was Aunt Sylvi's oldest son and my dad's cousin. I'm named after him. I guess I should start further back than that. Grandpa Gordano and Aunt Sylvi's husband, Uncle Sal, were brothers. Their dad brought the family over from Italy before the First World War. Uncle Joe was Aunt Sylvi and Uncle Sal's oldest boy. My dad tells me he was something else: handsome, funny, and a genuinely nice person. I found this letter in Aunt Sylvi's attic years ago. Luckily, she was still alive when I found it.

"According to Aunt Sylvi, in 1942 when Joe was eighteen years old, he met a young girl his age and they fell in love. Aunt Sylvi had never met her before and assumed she was new to the area. They were together nearly every minute of every day for about a month, then Joe was drafted to go to war. He wanted to marry her before he left. He talked it over with Aunt Sylvi. The girl had no family, so Aunt Sylvi offered to let her stay with her after Joe left for the war. Sylvi said she was a terrific girl, and she looked forward to having her in the family. So much so that she gave Joe a ring that had been in the family for years. She gave it to him to use as an engagement ring. Aunt Sylvi said when Joe proposed, the girl loved it. She loved it because it was different. It had a ruby, not a diamond like most engagement rings.

"Aunt Sylvi said, like the ring, the girl was different from the others as well. But Aunt Sylvi worried that there was so much they didn't know about her. She knew the girl loved Joe; that was certain. But there was something about her, something that seemed to be secret. Then one day, about a week before the wedding, she disappeared.

"Oh, poor Joe. That's a horrible story. Why are you telling me this?" Connie asked, puzzled.

"There is more," Joseph continued. "Joe never gave up on her. He waited and waited for her to return. He knew someone could not just walk away from a love like theirs. But then the day came when he had to leave for the war. He wrote her this letter and left it behind in hopes that she would come home while he was away. I want to read it to you now."

"Okay. I feel like I'm in a soap opera or something." Connie laughed awkwardly. "Are you just *trying* to make me cry?"

"Hang in there. I do have a point." Joseph smiled. "So, here's the letter." He began:

My dearest Gracie,

You left me as quickly as you came to me. I miss you, my darling, and I love you with all my heart. I know you will one day return to me, and although I will be gone, I will wait for you. I will marry you! No one can take away the love that we share.

I think about the day I found you, so scared and wide-eyed. Neither of us knowing quite how you got here. I listened for hours to the stories of your "time," so fast and disconnected. You said yourself that you never belonged there, and when you met me, you finally understood why. You belong with me.

Why did you run from me, my darling? Is it the war that scares you? Nothing would stop me from coming home to you, if I just knew you were here waiting for me. When you get this letter, my darling, you must write soon. I must know that you have returned to me. That you are waiting for me. That you will marry me.

I long for you every day I am not near you, my dear Grace. My dear, dear Grace Barsetti. The sound of your name makes my heart ache. I will come home to you. Please come home to me.

Always yours,
Joe

Connie sat and stared at Joseph. Tears spilled down her cheeks. She was speechless.

"I was right, wasn't I?" Joseph asked.

Connie nodded her head, still unable to speak.

"Grace is your mom, isn't she?" Again, she nodded.

"I knew it!" Joseph stood and waved the envelope in the air. "When I read this letter, and you said your mom grew up in that same house, I just knew it! When she was eighteen, she fell through the same closet you did and landed in the same closet you did! But she met my Uncle Joe in 1942! How unbelievable is that? I just knew she had to be your mother!" He continued to savor his victory for a few minutes longer until he realized that the eleven-year-old girl sitting in front of him needed him to finally be a grown-up.

"Ah, honey." Joseph slapped his forehead. "I'm an idiot. I'm sorry." He sat back down.

"What happened to him?" Constance asked in a small voice.

Joseph let out a heavy sigh. "He was killed in the war."

"Oh no!" She began to cry again.

Once more, Joseph knelt and held her. "What is it? Why are you crying?"

"It's just so sad. First, to think that she had such an incredible love, and then she lost it all of a sudden because of that dumb closet! And for him . . . Well, he thought she left him on purpose. And it's not that my mom isn't happy and in love now, because she is. She really is!" Connie sniffed and reached for another tissue. "But to think she was willing to stay shows she loved him that much. I mean, my first instinct was to find a way to go home. Sure, my mom was older and all when she time traveled, but she was willing to stay and leave her entire life behind because her love for him was so strong." She began to sob. "I just feel so bad for her." Connie shook her head sorrowfully. "My poor mother!"

CHAPTER 11

Sonny's Glasses

Connie sat dazed. Here she was on the sofa, with Joseph, in his office, just as she had been only days before in Aunt Sylvi's attic. But days before, Joseph was only twelve. Today he was a grown-up and had just told her that she was not the first to fall through Grandpa's mysterious closet.

Apparently, her mother had fallen through years ago when she was eighteen and had fallen in love with Joseph's uncle. This was before she met her dad, of course. Connie knew her mom loved her dad; there was no question there. But was it love at first sight like it was with Joe? She was sorry that her mother lost such an incredible love, but at the same time, if she hadn't, she would have never met her dad!

"This is so crazy," Connie finally said to Joseph.

"I had a feeling you would say that." He smiled warmly. "Can you stay for dinner?"

"No, I told my Aunt Jen that I would be home," Connie replied. "It's so weird. She was just getting to my house when I left to come find you. I think I came back from your house on the same day I fell through. I'm not really sure. Mom and Dad are in

Italy and won't be back for a while. When they get back, do you think I could bring Mom here to meet you and we could tell her about Joe and all of this together?"

"Are you sure? Wouldn't you rather do that on your own?" Joseph asked.

"No, I'm sure. Everything is easier when you are around." Connie knew she was looking at a grown man. But to her, he was still her twelve-year-old friend.

"Will you at least let me drive you home? We can throw your bike in the back of my truck. Oh, and I want to write down your address and phone number. I want it for myself, but then I also want to e-mail it to Sonny and Pete."

Connie laughed. "The other day I was in Aunt Sylvi's dining room, and I mentioned wishing I had access to the internet. You were like, 'What's that?' It was funny."

"I just can't imagine what that was like for you. Being back in time and all." Joseph handed Connie a sticky pad and a pen. "Put down your phone and address if you would."

"It was awesome. That's what it was like!" she said with a sigh. "Oh, and get this! I found Aunt Sylvi's ruby ring a couple of years ago in the closet! When I showed it to my mom, she just cried. Of course, I asked her if I could have it! I thought it was Grandma's!" Connie laughed. "Mom said no pretty quickly."

Joseph laughed too. "Aunt Sylvi would be glad it's in your family. I wish you could have been there when I found this letter. I told her that I thought Grace was your mother. I explained to her how I thought it was possible. I'm not sure how old she was. It was when we were moving her out of the big old house into the retirement home. I know she was more than ninety by then. Aunt Sylvi just closed her eyes and smiled. I think she was imagining you two together. As she smiled, tears ran down her cheeks. She really loved you, Connie."

"I loved her too." Constance wiped her eyes. "Now will you please stop making me cry?"

They both laughed.

"I can't remember why I'm holding these sticky notes," Connie said, chuckling.

"Address and phone number. E-mail if you have it!" Joseph reminded her.

"Got it!" She wrote it all down. "I really need to go. But I feel better knowing I can come back." She stood to give him a hug. "And I will take that ride home. Thanks."

"It's a deal. I just need to remember where I put my keys." He patted his pockets and glanced around the room.

"Hard to remember things now that you are old and all, is it?" Connie teased. She made herself laugh. "Hey, where is that picture Pete was talking about? I want to see it!"

"It's the big one over there." Joseph gestured toward the far wall. "It's really neat. He did it with his computer somehow with all the photos from that old camera of his. He gave it to me when I turned fifty. Can you believe that?" He laughed.

Connie wandered over and looked at it closely. It was made up of many small pictures. Somehow, across the top, several pictures spelled out the word "FRIENDSHIP."

"This is amazing! How did he do this?" she asked.

"I don't know. He can do some crazy stuff." Joseph joined her.

"These are great photographs of you guys! You three have been friends for so long. That's really neat!"

"Three? You'd better take a closer look there," Joseph said.

Connie took a step closer. She studied the many photos that made up the amazing collage.

"Oh my goodness! That's me! I'm in there!" she exclaimed, pointing to her own image. "I'm going to cry again!" She laughed a little. "That's us at the malt shop together! There's me in the attic! Here I am at the carnival. There's me with the purple giraffe I won and then lost! Ah, there's Sonny and me together." She frowned, trying to recall. "I don't remember taking that one. That's us together, and he's wearing his new glasses." She turned to Joseph. "Wait, that's not possible."

"Uh oh!" He put his arm around her shoulder and guided her away from the photograph. "I forgot about those."

"I don't get it." Connie was puzzled. "What pictures are those? How did Pete get a picture of me with Sonny wearing his new glasses? Did he do that with his computer? He didn't take that at Aunt Sylvi's. I would remember because I was just there!"

Joseph didn't say a word. He just looked at her strangely and jingled his keys.

"Joseph, Sonny's new glasses weren't ready until after I left," Connie insisted.

Silence.

"Joseph! The only way Pete could have gotten those pictures is if he took them at a different time. Which would mean . . . ?"

She looked at Joseph.

He sat back down on the edge of his desk and waited.

She sat down on the edge of a table and waited.

"Joseph?" Connie began to smile.

"Well . . ." Joseph smiled back. "Let's just say that 1959 wasn't our last adventure."

"What?" Connie was breathless. "You mean *I go back*?"

He nodded.

"What? No way! How many times do I go back? When do I go back next? Oh, I'm *so* excited! I have so many questions!" She was jumping around the office, waving her arms.

Jospeh chuckled. "I can see that! But let's talk in the truck. I need to get you home."

Connie followed Joseph down the stairs to his truck. She yelled goodbye to Sydney and her mom and realized she could hardly breathe.

"How about you slow down a little there, champ. Maybe take a few breaths." Joseph laughed.

"Whew! Okay! Yeah!" Connie took a few deep breaths. "I mean, come on! This is just crazy! Do we figure out how the closet works? Can I come whenever I want? When I get home, I'm going to kick and punch and body slam every wall in there!"

"All right, tough guy!" He couldn't stop smiling. "I don't think that's how it works. It just happens when it happens."

"Turn here at the weird mailbox and then go past the field," Connie directed.

"Wow that *is* weird. Did someone make that?" Joseph asked.

"I dunno." She shrugged. "You need to start slowing down. Okay, this one. Turn here."

Joseph pulled down her driveway and promptly grabbed her bike. He walked it down to the garage door, and when he looked back Connie was crying. "No, no, no!" he said, putting his hands on her shoulders. "Now you can come see me anytime you like!"

"It's not the same." She put her face in her hands and continued to cry.

"Aw, come here." Joseph pulled her into a hug. "Just be happy, my crazy girl. My crazy Connie." He closed his eyes and hugged her tight. He remembered that first time she appeared in Aunt Sylvi's closet so long ago. In that moment, he realized the young girl he was comforting was the best friend he had ever had.

"Okay!" Constance wiped her eyes. "No more crying. When Mom and Dad get home, we will have you over for dinner. Mom's no Aunt Sylvi, but she's an okay cook." She giggled.

"Sounds like a plan. You text or call me anytime!" Joseph couldn't believe how emotional he was feeling. "Now get inside; looks like rain!"

Connie smiled and ran toward the door, turning back to wave goodbye. She couldn't wait to get inside and explore her closet.

"Hi, honey!" Aunt Jen called as she heard Connie come in. "Dinner is almost ready."

"Okay, thanks! I'll be down in a sec." Connie answered as she ran into her room and plopped on her bed with a sigh. "I can't believe I go back!" she muttered to herself. "I cannot believe I go *back*! Crazy!"

**Enjoy this sample from 1960, the next
book in the *Crazy Connie's Closet* series.**

———— ❧ ————

C onnie looked in the long mirror, admiring
her new dress and the way her mom had
fixed her hair. Today was her twelfth birthday,
and she couldn't wait to go out to dinner to
celebrate. Proudly, she pranced into the living
room for the big reveal.

Dad picked her up and twirled her around,
announcing how beautiful she looked.

Anthony, unmoved by his sister's birthday,
asked if they could finally leave.

Mom clapped her hands, looked at Connie
lovingly, and said, "I think your new sandals
will compliment your dress better than those
fuzzy socks."

Connie laughed. "Agreed!" She held up
a wait-one-second finger and dashed to her
room. She spun expertly on the hardwood
floor in the slippery socks and then slid chaot-
ically into her closet, losing control. "Woah!"
She couldn't stop! Crash! Her hands slammed
onto the back wall . . . then it happened.

"Not noooooowwwwww!" she cried as she was pulled into a dark and dizzying tumble.

Thud! Yep. There it was . . . the cold, hard floor of Aunt Sylvi's fresh-smelling closet. "Crazy!" Connie sighed and laid there for a second to catch her breath.

Really? I've been so excited to come back, but right now? On my birthday? Really?

Suddenly there was a loud bang on the closet door. "What's going on in there?" a big, scary voice demanded.

Connie stumbled to her feet and peaked into the hallway. There stood Aunt Sylvi with a frying pan and spatula, ready to wallop whomever was inside.

Connie giggled. "Don't fry me up, Aunt Sylvi," she said, opening the door fully. "It's just me, Connie."

"Constance, dear!" The loud scary screamer returned to sweet Aunt Sylvi. "What a lovely surprise. I wasn't expecting you."

"Me neither, Aunt Sylvi." Connie laughed and immediately hugged her dear friend. "I've missed you guys so much." She looked up with a questioning gaze and added, "What year is it?"

Aunt Sylvi stepped back with a smile and said, "Oh sakes, dear. It's 1960."

About the Author

Janelle Otoya was a slow reader as a child, so books weren't a big thing for her—until she found Judy Blume and Beverly Cleary, who used humor in their writing. Then she was hooked.

Janelle's mom would shoo her and her sister, Joelle, off the front porch, where they enjoyed their books, to "get moving." They would head out on their bikes just like Connie and Joseph, exploring the neighborhood and visiting friends. They always knew when it was time to go back home when they heard the big, heavy brass bell with the long wooden handle. Their mom would step out on the porch and ring, and ring, and ring that thing. No matter where they were in the neighborhood, it could always be heard. Think of it as the cell phone of the 1970s.

Today, Janelle lives outside Kansas City with her husband, two grown children, and crazy dog, Frankie. She enjoys watching old musicals with her daughter, taking road trips with her husband, and baking.

www.ingramcontent.com/pod-product-compliance
Lightning Source LLC
Chambersburg PA
CBHW030830020726
47499CB00006B/2143